M C Joudrey

CHARLESWOOD ROAD

Stories

iUniverse, Inc.
Bloomington
At Bay Press
Toronto and Winnipeg

Charleswood Road
Stories

Copyright © 2011 M C Joudrey
Visit Matt Joudrey on line at www.mattjoudrey.com

All rights reserved. No part of this book may be used or reproduced by any means, graphic, electronic, or mechanical, including photocopying, recording, taping or by any information storage retrieval system without the written permission of the publisher except in the case of brief quotations embodied in critical articles and reviews.

This is a work of fiction. All of the characters, names, incidents, organizations, and dialogue in this novel are either the products of the author's imagination or are used fictitiously.

iUniverse books may be ordered through booksellers or by contacting:

iUniverse
1663 Liberty Drive
Bloomington, IN 47403
www.iuniverse.com
1-800-Authors (1-800-288-4677)

Because of the dynamic nature of the Internet, any Web addresses or links contained in this book may have changed since publication and may no longer be valid. The views expressed in this work are solely those of the author and do not necessarily reflect the views of the publisher, and the publisher hereby disclaims any responsibility for them.

ISBN: 978-1-4620-0673-1 (pbk)
ISBN: 978-1-4620-0674-8 (ebk)

Printed in the United States of America

iUniverse rev. date: 3/25/2011

Cover design and interior art plates by the author
Cover photograph by Alana Brooker
At Bay Press is an independent, creator owned, Canadian imprint

For Jeff and Paul

Contents

Erik 1
   Candy Floss and Jumping Bugs . . . 5

Appointment 9
   Staying Between the Two 12

The Last Dartmoors of Devon 15
   Only the Dead Will Rest 18

Reflections of a Dying American Cigarette 21
   Untitled 23

Night Plane 25
   When 30

Thing 33
   Damned Silverfish 46

Through a Window Small 47

Understanding the Architect 49
   The Mustang 54

Plastic Query 55
   Elementary Weather 57

Charleswood Road 59

They were all here in the forest

Erik

THE MORNING AIR FELT GOOD. It brushed past Erik's face through his prison bars. He woke and couldn't remember much from the day before. He still felt groggy and allowed himself a yawn. He was lucky, he thought, to at least be outdoors; so many others served their time indoors. He had been restless and hadn't been sleeping well which was why he was fairly sure the guards had slipped something into his food. The meals came in meagre sizes and were barely edible even for him. He'd lost weight. That was expected. He looked his body over: he looked weak and could see the prominent outline of his rib cage and sunken chest. He'd always been lean and displayed powerful muscle definition, but now his bones appeared too close to the surface. This saddened him. His sentence was one he was not sure he'd survive.

The new day was breaking earlier than usual and Erik could already feel the sun's warmth on his back. He paced about his cell. He was thirsty and hadn't been left any food yesterday and there was none so far today. The water he'd been given two days ago was almost depleted. He couldn't see any guards at all and he wondered if whatever they had put in his food had kept him asleep all through yesterday.

The complex was quiet and felt empty. Something was wrong. His instincts had always been very keen; honed after years of experience dealing with the most cunning men on Earth and living in a land allowing little forgiveness for error. He wondered where everyone was and if they were even coming back. Where had all the guards gone? Where was the Pink Skinned Man? The Pink Skinned Man was someone whose name no one spoke and who had done terrible things to him, things he would never forget. The Pink Skinned Man told everyone what to do and they listened. The Pink Skinned Man watched him closely, afraid Erik may try to escape. He would look into Erik's cell and stare at him grinning with his rotten corn-coloured teeth. Erik would look right back at him. He would not be made afraid, after all he was a King where he came from. This angered the Pink Skinned Man, who relished the fear he struck in his guards. Then he would do things to Erik to show he was stronger than Erik, smarter than him, better than him. Though no matter what terrible things the Man would do, Erik would never show fear and kept his pride. For Erik was a King who had been abducted while he slept, by men with unique weapons far superior to those Erik had faced in the past. Cowards, he thought silently. I will have my revenge.

Now Erik was alone and the complex looked empty, devoid of its busy population. He wondered if he was the only one left. He couldn't see any of the other cells so it was hard to tell if others had been left behind. There was not a single sound from the other captives or inhabitants in the complex and this led Erik to believe he was positively alone. Alone. He thought to himself about the soft spot he'd discovered in the cell flooring and how he was sure he might be able to break through and with some digging he might win his freedom. He would wait a while longer, until late afternoon, to see if anyone would return and then he'd consider the idea again. In the meantime, he drank some water, leaving the last of it for later. For now he would try to get some rest.

The sun was high in the afternoon sky and the cell bars cast striped shadows onto the floor of Erik's cell and across his body as he sat, arms folded, looking out into silent emptiness. The late afternoon sun was getting hot. Erik examined the weak spot in his cell's flooring. He knew that the time had come to attempt an escape. He was alone, his only companion the eerie silence of the complex. There was an odour attached to the air now but Erik could not place what it was. He moved towards the weak spot in the floor and looked down at it. It shouldn't be too hard to break through. He wasn't looking forward to the digging though. He wondered if this was why the Pink Skinned Man watched him so closely. He must have known of the weak floorboards and that escape would be easy for anyone if given the chance.

Erik made short work of the flooring. Although making a hole large enough for him to slip through wasn't difficult, the fierce heat from the growing afternoon sun caused his thirst to flare. He decided to finish the last of his water before the dig. There wasn't much but enough to wet his dry mouth sufficiently.

The digging took him about twenty minutes. Once Erik was free he stood a moment to catch his breath and looked into the empty cell. He hadn't been there long but he would never forget what had happened to him in this place. He turned to face the open courtyard of the complex and assess his surroundings, looking for an opening or somewhere to crawl through. The perimeter walls were too high to climb, nor did he have the strength. Erik noticed the front gate was ajar. He thought this strange as he hadn't noticed the gate being open from within the confines of his cell. He slowly and quietly made his way towards the large gate doors. He took a quick peek through the doors, carefully checking for any signs of life. There were none, nothing except the strange odour in the air. Erik could see the muddy road winding its way to the left and forest in front of him. He didn't sense any danger so he left the complex and ran swiftly towards the trees. He'd be safer in the forest than along the road. Once inside the tree line, he turned and looked back at the complex for only a moment, then continued into the dense foliage.

Erik had been walking for over an hour at a good pace. The odour in the air had been growing stronger and he now knew what the smell was that he couldn't previously place. It was death. He heard the birds of carrion first, arguing greedily. Then he saw them: they where everywhere. He now knew where the guards were. They were all here in the forest with their weapons in hand, dead and disfigured from strange wounds. Predators were feasting on the rotting flesh. The birds shot questioning glances at him but were not the least bit afraid of him. It was apparent they felt there was enough here for everyone. Erik left the black winged creatures to their grisly business and waded through the awful death. His mind weary, he almost didn't hear the gurgling noise coming from a figure sitting against a large stone. It was the Pink Skinned Man. He was alive and looked at Erik. He had a sickly smile on his face and blood slowly oozed from the corner of his mouth.

"It's you," he said in his crude language that Erik did not always entirely understand.

"I knew you'd escape if I turned my back. I told them..." he choked on a laugh.

"You want to kill me don't you? I can see you want vengeance."

It was true Erik had wanted to kill this man for all the things he'd done to him.

"Well go ahead you disgusting..." he hacked and coughed, his death rattle approaching. "Indulge yourself..."

Erik couldn't understand his words. He approached the dying man, bringing his face only inches from his tormenter's. He could smell the sick scent of fear bleeding from the man's pores. The Pink Skinned Man looked into his eyes, and incredulously thought he could see a smile on Erik's face. Then Erik backed away and left him to his fate, making for the deep forest.

After some time he came to recognize his surroundings. He was getting close to home. Erik's ears twitched then perked up as he heard a rustling in the underbrush. In front of him appeared a tiger. Brash and unafraid, the tiger climbed a large jagged slice of granite and let out a powerful roar. Erik stared at the compelling beast standing majestically upon the stone slab. She was beautiful. He knew the beast. He knew her intimately. She was his Queen. She was his mate. He roared more powerfully than she, despite his fatigue. He was King and he was home.

Candy Floss and Jumping Bugs

He had a brick,
That's what he called it anyway
And a bag of blue and pink floss,
Nostalgia and childhood memories,
Suffocating in cheap poly.

The field was so very green
And damp.
Blades grew lovingly between my toes.
The sky one perfect blue
And nothing else.

He had a knife,
But it was small,
That was like him.
He slit the paper wrapping,
Then carefully laid out his tiny explosive prizes,
All over the ground around us.

I was on my back
He let me touch him,
The floss,
It was sticky and warm and soft.
Then hot, everything got hot.

I put pink floss in my mouth,
And my fingers,
Became useful.

I didn't understand everything,
He pretended to,
I liked that he did.

I don't remember certain things.
The lighter,
My eyes were closed,
Feeling.

I do remember the jumping bugs,
A thousand colourful Chinese orgasms,
Dancing, singing, snapping with our rhythm.
They burnt through their powder,
So did we.

He smiled at her but did not say hello

Appointment

THOSE FIRST FEW SIPS WERE so gratifying. The woman stood squarely on the street corner in her faded viridian sundress and tried in vain to keep her bobbed hair from sticking to the fresh lipstick on her lips while managing careful mouthfuls from the folded opening of her coffee cup. She'd decided to rise early this grey morning despite the overcast sky because the weather lady said there'd be sun if one was willing to exercise patience up until maybe one o'clock that afternoon. The woman liked the sun and what's more, she liked the smell and taste of strong coffee. She liked both so much that she thought she might be able to spend the rest of her life waiting for the sun to graciously appear if her coffee would last that long. She knew though that she was required elsewhere and she hadn't applied her lipstick for nothing so she stepped free from the curb. A horn honked callously at her and she jumped back. Her skirt had plumped like an open umbrella from the gusting wind hurled by the car as it swooped past. This is why she never went outside without Rosa, she remarked to herself as she glared with frayed nerves at the auto as it disappeared into traffic. How silly to have forgotten her early childhood rules of looking both ways before crossing the street.

She carefully crossed and then walked six blocks at a steady but leisurely pace. She was in no rush. She watched the other early risers as they passed by her. Some, like her, had coffees in their hands, others looked tired and weary and some looked late and rushed towards their destination. The smooth yet cool air brushed against her face but the afternoon sun would soon help raise the temperature a few degrees warmer. She finished her coffee and deposited it in the receptacle outside her destination. She entered the office building through the large revolving door, which swished around as she entered the welcome lobby. The woman approached the desk and was greeted by the receptionist.

"May I help you?"

"I have an appointment with Doctor Landau."

"Oh, you're early. Have a seat and I'll let the Doctor know you've arrived."

"Thank you."

The woman sat down and looked at the magazines strewn on the coffee table in the waiting room. She didn't care for any of the subject matter; still she selected a copy that had something to do with gardening and thumbed through the pages thoughtlessly. She set the magazine down and decided it didn't interest her at all.

The voice of the receptionist summoned her and the woman returned obediently to the reception desk.

"The Doctor will see you now," the receptionist pointed to the right hallway.

The woman remembered her last visit down the left hallway where she was made to wear one of those terrible robes and asked a barrage of questions.

Doctor Landau greeted her pleasantly in the hallway. He smiled at her but did not say hello and she did the same. They entered a room together and the Doctor sat on one side of a white-topped table and the woman sat on the other side.

"Well now, thank you for coming in for this quick visit. How are you feeling today?" The Doctor opened his folder and pushed the top button on his pen, holding it poised above the paper.

"Fine, thank you Doctor," the woman replied calmly with firm eye contact.

"This is good news. Have you given any thought with regards to my suggestion from our last visit?" He hesitated in wait of her response before jotting anything down on paper.

"Yes, I should like to try gardening. It seems rather nice." She smiled sincerely.

"Gardening?"

"Yes," came her affirmation.

"Well now, this is an excellent idea." His pen scrawled across the paper and he looked up at the woman again. "Have you found anything you like besides coffee?"

"Yes, the weather lady said it would be sunny today and I think I'll spend the day walking and enjoying the sun."

"Well now, I am very pleased to hear this. I think that should about wrap today's session. Oh, how is Rosa?"

"Who?"

The doctor's mouth formed a brief smile as he wrote a final note in the folder, tore off a page from his prescription pad and handed it to her. They both got up from their chairs at the same time and the Doctor led the woman back to the reception counter, smiled again, and waved as the woman walked away. The Doctor watched as the revolving doors continued to spin once she had exited though them. From his office, he could see people going about their days beneath the warm rays of sunlight.

Staying Between the Two

I have a friend who's clever.
He moves like tobacco smoke and lasts just as long.

I have another friend who ekes out painful smiles.
He's thin and reads personal ads with intent to follow up.
No, really.

They've never met.
I'm different people with each.

With my clever friend I'm on safari and hunt sex.
I dance sloth-like in a red and black jungle,
Eat words and trade moments like ivory.

With my thin friend I lie a lot.
I wait impatiently for my turn.
I speak and ask questions. I don't care for the answers.

I don't think either will ever meet my parents.

Neither broke their gaze

The Last Dartmoors of Devon

THE SUN HAD SET SOME time ago on the moor, but there was still warmth in the air. Gerald sat on the porch smoking his black-lipped pipe. He could hear the trees relaxing their branches in preparation for the imminent night. The sweet breeze reminded Gerald of when he was a boy, growing up in these parts. Devon unfortunately had changed over the years and now in the final few seasons of his life, he spent his remaining time at his cottage in the moorlands.

Gerald lived alone. He never had any guests or callers at his door. His son Arthur was the only person who ever visited him and as Gerald's health worsened in the last year, Arthur's visits had become infrequent. He was a stubborn old man and when his son had approached him with papers to sell his home in Devon, Gerald spewed tobacco-stained saliva all over the first page.

"Let the damn thing rot! Devon proper is poison. The moor is the last place on Earth with any soul left in it." He leaned in closer to his son. "You know my boy, the Dartmoor still walk this land." Gerald nodded in agreement with his own words and eased back into his chair.

"Dad, will you stop talking nonsense about those bloody ponies!" His son was furious.

Gerald's face flushed crimson and he yanked the pipe out from his lips, waving it in the air. "You'll hold your tongue and speak with respect in my presence!"

Arthur recoiled. Even at his overripe age, Gerald could still instill fear in his son. The boy, now a man, rose from his father's presence, shook his head and said nothing, making his way for home.

"Young fool," Gerald muttered once his son was out of sight.

He re-lit his pipe and took three heavy pulls on the stem. A rich plume of grey smoke filled the air around him. He looked out on the moor. The evening moon was low and almost full; a soft eerie glow blanketed the land, however one could still see for quite a distance. Gerald watched in silence as the first of them appeared.

"Hello, old friend," he whispered the words in his mind only.

The pony moved over the crest of the hill and into full view. The creature was a female. Her coat was black and shone like the surface of the lake beneath the moon's delicate light. Her mane was long, unruly.

Gerald and the beast met gazes. They would do this each evening; stare at each other in silent understanding. They both weren't long for this world and had an unspoken agreement. The others would eventually come. Gerald had been a part of this ritual for many years.

He reached into the inside pocket of his wool jacket and removed a bottle of pills. It was that time. He took out two light yellow pills and reached for his water, took a mouthful and threw his head back to swallow. He waited a few moments for his stomach to settle and then looked back out on the moor. The Dartmoors had gone. He got up, turned off the porch light and went inside.

The next night brought the same visitation; first the black female, then the rest of the Dartmoors would come silently and Gerald would light his pipe. They would watch each other, then the ponies would graze the moor in the moonlight. Gerald lived for his evenings with these animals although eventually he would start to grow tired and it was then he knew it was time for his pills. He would take them each night at the prescribed time and the Dartmoors would leave as though they knew he would be making his way to bed.

It was August when things changed for the first time in all the years Gerald had been on the moor. The black female had a routine. She would arrive first and remain at a distance while the others waited. On this night though, she left the safety of the tree line and trotted slowly towards the porch. She slowed to a walk about twenty feet from the porch. She looked at Gerald and him at her, as they had always done. Neither broke their gaze. The bold advance of the pony did not surprise Gerald. They had known each other for many years. She would only become bolder now that things had changed, although Gerald knew it all along to be true. The other ponies did not come that night. She turned and made her way towards the trees while Gerald watched her go. He took his pills and went to bed.

The next night Gerald sat on his porch, pipe dangling from his mouth and stared out at the crest of the hill. He waited patiently. Tonight was the night he'd been waiting for all this time.

Eventually she emerged out of the trees, coming up over the crest of the hill and making her way towards Gerald at a calm even trot. When she stopped a few feet from the porch, Gerald was no longer sitting but standing. They looked at each other for a time and then Gerald turned his gaze out at the moor. The others had congregated along the crest of the hill. Gerald nodded evenly to no one in particular and made his way down the porch steps. The pony raised her head and Gerald laid a hand upon the beautiful black creature's mane.

"Okay," he said. And that was all. It was the only time he had let her hear his voice. She made no sound and remained silent, as always. She turned and started to slowly make her way towards the others, stopping to look back at Gerald. He understood and followed her like she wanted him to.

* * *

It was a few days later when they discovered the body. Arthur had tried to call to see if his father would reconsider signing the papers but received no answer. Arthur had asked Dr. Wortham to join him on the trip out to the moor, even though he knew the doctor would not be of much use.

He looked at his father who was sitting in his chair on the porch, eyes open, looking out at the moor. His father looked incredibly peaceful and more at ease than Arthur thought he'd ever seen him while he was alive.

"He would always talk about the Dartmoor ponies when I visited him," remarked Arthur, as he looked upon his father sitting there.

"Dartmoors, really? Hasn't been a Dartmoor on this land for almost twenty-five years. The last of the breed died in captivity at least twelve years ago." The doctor stood a moment in reflection. "Sad really, they were beautiful creatures."

"I know," said Arthur quietly, almost to himself. He turned and placed his hands on the railing of the porch, steadying himself, and looked out onto the moor. That is when he noticed something on the grass below and went down the steps to fetch it. About ten feet or so from the porch, Arthur reached down and picked up an unopened plastic container of his father's pills.

Only the Dead Will Rest

A man takes a shower
Puts on a suit and goes to work, recording his mileage
He comes home, warms up leftovers and watches the television
Makes paltry conversation with his wife
After a while he goes to bed and the alarm clock and routine are reset for tomorrow

Another man ties his shoe with a broken lace
He pulls yesterday's newspaper around his body and shuts his eyes
He will eat nothing and witness another man capture and eat a rat
He urinates in a city planter box while statistics look but don't see
Numbers without faces

A girl at a party smokes a joint
It is her first time
Her eyes glaze
John approaches her and she can't find the right words
He is confused and walks away with friends
She will have sex with Danny an hour later

Another girl does not drink
She studies and never goes to parties
She achieves top honours upon graduation
A job is offered and she works 14 hours a day
This will go on for 15 years
At the age of 35 she will look 55 and feel 65
She will be rich

A dog cools his belly on the concrete steps
The afternoon sun begins to creep slowly into his shade
He is unaware
He watches his master
Who toils beneath the same blazing sky as he cuts the lawn

A woman fills her car with fuel
The price is $1.17 a litre
She watches another woman on a bicycle ride by as the fuel pump clicks off
The woman pulls the nozzle from her vehicle
She pinches the fat at her waist
A bike could help with that

Reflections of a Dying American Cigarette

It's true I've killed; I've taken a man's life, but who does not know of someone who has done the same? Oh, sure, maybe it was in the name of country or freedom or the acquisition of mineral deposits, but is that any better than taking a life in the name of personal pleasure and satisfaction? I ask this be contemplated as I continue to expire.

My smoker has taken a drag from me and placed me lovingly in the ashtray near his coffee. I do my best to burn slowly and build a proud silken wave of smoke around me. I am careful not to ash too quickly as I am aware my life is coming to its end. I am confident that I should be able to provide at least two more healthy draws before I extinguish to the filter. Then I will leave my legacy in the hands of my anxious brothers who still faithfully remain in the comfortable package for their climactic moment to arrive.

It feels like a lifetime ago that I was lit by the butane lighter and felt my smoker take his first puff from me. Such a terrible and wonderful feeling all at once to know that with each inhalation from me into my smoker's lungs I am performing my one task that will ultimately take my life. Is it so unfair that I should do the same to him?

I like watching my smoker speak. At this moment he is engrossed in a meaningful conversation with a woman in whom he appears to have great interest. So many of the world's most important conversations have been had over a cigarette. It's the smoking that induced the conversation and nurtured it to fruition. Imagine, if you will, all the conversations human beings might not have had if smoking was not readily available.

I have heard from other cigarettes, back in the early stages of our birth as we rolled along the assembly line at the factory before being packaged, that a very gratifying human experience is to smoke immediately after pleasurable sexual intercourse. This is of course something I will never get to experience, as my fate has been ordained and my one life experience will play out here at this café.

I watch my smoker's hand slowly reach down for me while he continues to make eye contact with the woman in front of him. His movements with regard to my life are subconscious, machine-like, and I feel terribly neglected. A deep sorrow is realized; one of my final drags will be so very nonchalant. Still, I will do everything I must to fill my smoker's lungs with pleasure and help spur his intimate conversation.

Once I am returned to the ashtray I realize I may not be able to perform for one final pull on the filter. The previous one was too deep and long and left little of my precious tobacco. Still, with great effort I will try to hold out for one more final moment of satisfaction.

I remember when I was first packaged and how lovely it felt to be part of such a large family. I doubt any family could be closer than we were. I can still hear the cheers of my brothers as I had been selected to be the next in our smoker's life. They were all so proud of me. I am proud of myself too; I've worked hard for my smoker. I'll not feel guilty if I should cause his health any harm. Do not a cheeseburger and fries kill just as often? I would consider myself to be much more satisfying than any fast food greasy burger.

I look up one last time at my smoker who has forgotten where I lay and has not taken notice that I am about to expire. I feel lonely and desperate in my last moments and wish he would at least begin to reach for me even though I have nothing left to offer. Please, reach for me! Yes! I see his hand approaching. Thank you.

"Hmm, damn thing's finished. You don't mind if I...?"
"Not at all."
"Great."
Flick! Flick!
"Mmm, so as I was saying..."

Untitled

I check the bowl
Empty
Always half empty

Sit around the apartment
My perch on the 28th floor
Watch the ants
Tomorrow at 8:00 a.m.
I'll be one too

Not so bad
I get to do stuff
Thanks to the pittance
It adds up

Time erodes the soles
Unravels the laces
Silences the tongue
Can swallow the soul

But the sun comes up
Each day
The damn thing
Keeps on coming
I guess I can too

Plus I like seeing it
Each day
Somehow always worth it

Soon, he thought

Night Plane

The plane was leaving the tarmac at 6:45 p.m. and Donald slid the vinyl blind open so he could look out the window. The sun was just sinking below the horizon and fleshy hues dashed softly across the clouded sky. Soon, he thought, they would be above the clouds and he would leave the colours and the city behind him.

Donald was sick. In fact, he was dying. He still had some time; the disease was really only just starting to progress. He had his mobility and lucidity, but he didn't know for how long, which is why he left.

Donald had purchased a one-way ticket. He sat in coach even though he could more than afford executive class. He was going to see his daughter, Jennifer. He hadn't seen her in four years, since the wedding. He had never been much of a father but that was when things were at their worst. Now on the last few miles of his life, he would go to see if there was any redemption for him at all in her eyes. He had neglected her terribly when Annette was still alive. Annette, would she be waiting for him? At least he had been a faithful husband. He never betrayed her, but he was just never there.

I think she understood, Donald thought, wincingly. He was thinking of her in her last days and what she'd said to him.

"Don't lose your window to be her father."

Then she died with dignity like someone like her would. Donald looked out the plane window. The sky was a deep, dark blue with a few stubborn, fading colours. It looked like a bruise and reflected his pain. The attendant touched his arm.

"Would you care for a beverage, sir?"

"Water."

"Of course."

The attendant poured and passed then moved the trolley to the next aisle. Donald took a small sip from the cup and looked back out the window. The sky's colours had vanished. Things change that quickly. Now the night was nothing but darkness. Donald reclined his seat slightly and tilted his head back against the headrest. He would try to sleep. He thought about the first time Jennifer slept in the new house when he and Annette brought her home from the hospital. Donald couldn't remember the delivery, the birth or anything else from the hospital that day but he could remember with remarkable accuracy watching how his newborn daughter slept that night. He sat beside the crib in the antique wooden chair his wife had purchased only a month before for the room.

"This is for when you want to watch her," Annette's distant voice replayed softly in his ear.

A foolish extravagant purchase he had thought at the time, as he watched his child sleep and he himself began to doze. He had never since known a peace like that night.

The plane was quiet now. The attendant had finished her concessions and was somewhere in the back. The other passengers were mostly asleep though a few read books or magazines. He felt alone now, not lonely. There's a difference between the two. He was alone and could finally be truly honest with himself. He probably wouldn't even get in the front door. He might have a little under a minute to explain himself before she closed it on him. He had hurt her with what he'd said at the wedding.

"Thanks for coming, Dad. I know you're busy."

"I am these days darling, as always. Is this him?"

"Dad, meet Jim."

"A pleasure to meet you sir."

"What do you do with your time, son?"

"I'm in construction. A foreman actually."

"I see. I suppose you'll need my help often then with issues of finance."

"Dad!"

"It's all right, Jenny. Mr. Kroft, can I get you a drink?"

"I can find my way. Nice meeting you, John."

It was no surprise his daughter had asked Jim's father to make a speech at her wedding rather than him. That choice stung him, despite the endless vodka sodas he had consumed. She had done the right thing; at best he would have embarrassed her but more likely worse. Donald had passed the point of no return at nine that evening and the last thing he would remember from his only child's wedding night were her last words to him. He had just entered the elevator of the ballroom to leave and she held the doors open, just as they were clamping shut.

"I have forgiven so much because I believed you were in pain over mom. I can't forgive you for this one Dad, I just can't."

And the elevator doors closed. This was the last time she had spoken to him.

The seatbelt sign sounded and the lighting came on in the cabin. The captain made a brief announcement that they would be landing soon and the local time was 7:45 p.m. They had gained two hours in the air. Donald set his watch to the correct time and stood up to get his bag in the overhead bin. He reached for the latch and felt a hot wave wash over him; he suffered a powerful bout of vertigo and lost his balance. Another passenger caught him as he fell and helped him back to his feet.

"You alright buddy?"

"I … I think so, just need a little fresh air is all."

The passenger lifted Donald's bag out of the bin, pulled the luggage handle up for him and handed it to him.

Donald had not checked any other luggage and made his way outside the airport. The air outside was cool and there was a breeze which did wonders to restore his vitality. This sudden resurgence of energy made him aware of how nervous he was. He was only a few short kilometres from his daughter. He hailed a cab and gave the driver the address.

Donald rubbed his hands together in the back seat, trying to stay calm. What would he say when she opened the door?

The cab pulled up to the house and Donald paid the driver. It wasn't until the brake lights of the cab had disappeared over the hill that Donald realized he was alone and hadn't moved an inch from where he had stepped out of the cab. She was in there and he was afraid of being rejected by her, his only child, his daughter, a woman whose life he was mostly absent for and whom he barely knew. She probably hated him and thought of him only in moments of weakness and anger, he thought to himself. His whole life, his wealth, the money, everything but Annette felt like one big regret. He could leave now, walk away and no one would know he was ever there or know that he was a coward even in his last moment of real living. In his gut he knew his daughter would not speak with him and would close the door in his face. He could feel that awful feeling already, but he loved her. He'd always loved her from that first night he watched her sleep and every day after he loved her, even though his actions may have not reflected this.

He stepped forward towards the door.

His thoughts pulled at him to such a painful degree that he felt physically hurt from the mental stress as he managed his way to the front door. He made a fist to knock. He hesitated again just before his knuckles struck the surface of the door; he had thought of nothing to say. He clenched his fist so tightly that his knuckles turned white as he rapped on the door. He took a step back absently and waited.

The latch on the door turned and Donald felt his heart become swollen in his chest and beat on him like an eight-ounce glove.

When the door opened it was his daughter who spoke first.

"What are you doing here?" She looked more surprised at first but then he could see irritation flit into her eyes.

"I came to see you." He sounded meek, not like himself and feared his lack of confidence would only further her annoyance.

"Why?"

He looked at her without saying anything for only a moment. He wanted to take the easy way out, deal the death card. But he didn't, he didn't want her back that way. He wanted her to forgive him or at the very least let him tell her he was sorry.

"I got on a plane this evening because I wanted to see you. I didn't plan it, I just had to do it."

"Well, you've seen me, now I think you should go."

He had lost her already but was not ready to give up, not after making it this far.

"You know I'm an asshole, I know I'm an asshole. I was engrossed with my career when I was working. I made a lot of money that now disgusts me. I miss your mother. I was a terrible husband and an even worse father. I'm no good and I've always known it."

Donald looked at his daughter. He had experienced his first moment of true humility and that was enough. She said nothing. He said nothing. He turned and made his way down the steps of the porch.

"Mr. Kroft?

Donald turned and found Jim standing behind his daughter in the doorway. He was an honest and decent man who ensured his daughter's happiness and safety, when Donald could not. Jennifer looked up at her husband; he stood much taller than she and was offering her his confidence in the moment.

"Would you like to see your grandson?"

"Yes, I would." His lack of hesitation in answering surprised his daughter more than it did himself.

Jim invited him in. The interior of the home was warm and felt lived-in. The furnishing was modest but cared for. Donald could see a small fireplace burning hardwood in the living room. He was proud of his daughter and her honest achievements. They didn't need him but he would still offer the papers he'd brought. Jennifer watched her father as he absorbed his surroundings. She softened a little, sensing his vulnerability.

Upstairs the three of them entered a quiet room. The room was familiar, so much so that Donald felt immediately at ease.

"Would you like me to wake him?" asked his daughter.

Donald looked at the small child sleeping soundly in the crib. He could see himself in his daughter's work. He looked over at her; his eyes were red and heavy.

"If I could just sit for a while, you know, and watch him…" Donald trailed off, not really sure if he would be granted this small favour, or if he actually deserved it.

Jim went and fetched a chair and set it beside the crib. The two young parents left the room and Donald stood there for a moment, a small tear passing across his smiling lips. He walked towards his sleeping grandchild and took a seat in his wife's antique wooden chair.

When

Inside the walls of the Forbidden City
Having tea
The fragrance of the Hanging Gardens of Babylon
Under the cypress trees

I know that all of this will never be.

That old man in Georgia
Our last night in Alexandria
The oranges in Seville
The lost soul of the Barrier Reef

There was that, wasn't there?

And time. Always time.
Outside in the October rain
That final maple leaf falling
Joining the others among the detritus

Waiting for your plane to leave.

If you ever make your way back
I will forgive the promises you've made
I won't forget your moments of generosity
Nor your frequent cruelty

The nights we spent driving aimlessly.

I think you tried.
I'll say you did.
I'll tell them everything I should
But we both know you were mostly no good.

So I'll wish you well
Watch for your debut
While they all drink and smile with you,
And you'll always be the person I only knew.

No man should ever know

Thing

"If I tell the truth about that night, you won't believe me," said the man from across the table at which we sat. He was dressed in a grey hooded shirt and spoke with a smooth Yorkshire accent.

He had only arrived five minutes earlier and had kept me waiting an hour. When asked why he was so late, he said he'd been outside watching the place since nine o'clock. I'd asked what he was watching for and he shook his head and ran his soiled hands through his greasy hair. He was nervous, that much was plain, and his alertness was unsettling. I signalled to the waitress for another round while holding up two fingers, thinking a drink might do him some good. He slid further into his seat and a small shadow covered half of his face, for which he seemed appreciative. The beverages arrived and he stared at the bottle of lager like it might be filled with coiled snakes.

"Just a lager," I said, trying to ease his trepidation.

He reluctantly put both hands around the bottle and shakily brought it to his lips. He took a half-hearted swig and his eyes flitted about the room as he did so.

"Why don't we start right from the beginning and the reason you felt you should contact me."

"You're a policeman, a detective. Am I right?"

"That's right, a Senior Detective," I replied, holding my lager patiently before my lower lip.

He slid out from the safety of the shadows enhanced by the poor lighting of the pub for just a moment, enough for me to make out his features a bit better. There was no doubt that this man wore his life on his face; the lines around his eyes and mouth told stories of their own.

"I have a friend you once helped and she spoke of you often and quite fondly. She said you're not like other policemen. She said that you don't just listen but you'll pay attention too."

"Who might your friend be?" I asked, still questioning why I'd ventured out for this.

"Carol," he answered meekly, looking down at his trembling fingers.

Carol was a convicted prostitute with an eye for vein candy. I had once done my best to help her get clean and had turned a few familiar stones to get her a terrible job that paid her poorly. It was better than what she was used to and it was the best I could do. She wasn't that smart, but she had managed to stay clean for over a year.

"So you know Carol and she told you to come see me. What about?" I asked, doing my best to hide my already apparent impatience.

"She's dead."

"Who's dead?" I asked, although I already knew the answer.

"Carol." He looked sullenly away from me when he replied.

I took a moment to collect my thoughts. Carol's dead. Surely I knew it would happen someday so why was it so surprising to me?

"Did anyone report it?"

"No." He had still not been able to make eye contact with me.

"Was it an overdose?"

"It wasn't drugs," he replied, shaking his head while focusing on the bottle in front of him.

"Well, where is she?" I shouted at him, leaning across the table with my arms outstretched. "You better start talking with clear and concise answers or I'll put cuffs on you and take you out of here right now!"

He stared right through me with his hollow grey eyes and seemed not the least bit rattled by my sudden abrasive outburst. He wasn't at all afraid of me, yet he seemed so very afraid of something else.

"That's why I'm here detective. I was there the night she died. I was her friend, maybe the only one she had besides you." His gaze cooled my temper enough to hear him further.

"You have to understand, I am not even sure she's dead. My God, I wasn't even supposed to be there, but she insisted."

I kept mum, waiting to see if he'd make more sense.

"I was going to meet some pals from the east end. I'd heard of a party and thought I might see a woman I'd met a few weeks earlier." He took a sip from his bottle of lager then looked down at the label. "Carol came by my place that night before the party. Her eyes told of an unbelievable fear but her silence was even worse. It took me twenty minutes just to get her breathing normally."

"Was there some sort of trouble with a dealer?"

"I thought the same thing. I've seen her in a bad way many times before, but this was very different. It was like she'd seen, well, a ghost." He paused again to wet his mouth with drink, then turned and searched the rest of the pub with his eyes.

"Who are you looking for?" I asked sternly.

"I know how this appears detective. I know. A man you've never met calls you, asking to meet you and then tells you someone is dead, someone who you know. It's just so hard to get myself together when what I know, what I saw can't really be explained. It's not…"

"Look, just try to calm down. I'm listening and I want to know what's happened so we can figure this out. But I need you to be very straightforward with me and tell me exactly what has transpired. Take a deep breath and start with when Carol arrived at your flat."

My faith in him and my sincere words seemed to have settled him slightly. He had another sip of lager and then took a deep breath, as if he was going to regurgitate the entire story in one sentence.

"Take it slow. I'm listening," I said, trying to reassure him.

"When Carol arrived at my flat I didn't take her seriously, not at first. She was hysterical, almost flailing her limbs like some kind of Bellevue Betty. Then I saw the blood on her." He stopped momentarily and made eye contact with me. From the half shadow that obscured him, he looked maniacal and in that moment I felt my skin grow cold. I took a drink as he continued. "It wasn't her blood, that much I could ascertain. After I calmed her and cleaned her up a little I managed to get her talking, although she made little sense."

"What did she say?"

He looked at me and his eyes silently scolded my interruption. As much as I hated his cryptic delivery, it was obvious things would have to continue on his terms in order to hear the entire tale.

"She told me she'd seen a monster."

I rolled my eyes. I was now confident she must've been high. What a waste of time this was. I'd get the report in the morning and it would read part time hooker-junkie found face down, a park needle still in arm.

"Ah, detective I can tell I've lost you. Maybe she wasn't a friend to you. But to her, well, she considered you a saint. Shall I finish or have I wasted your time?" He read my expression perfectly and I felt momentarily guilty, despite the ridiculous direction the story was heading in.

"I'm sorry, as an officer of the law I don't put much stock in monster theories."

"I didn't believe her either, but she was scared enough to rattle me, so I agreed to hear her out."

"I'm still listening. But let's speed it up some, okay?"

"I'll do my best." He fiddled with his bottle nervously, like it was going to take some great effort to carry on. "Like I said, I didn't believe her either, but there was the blood. I asked her whose blood it was. She said it was Terri's."

That's another name I knew well. Terri was a hooker who had been working those streets before most girls had their license.

"As you probably knew detective, Terri and Carol sometimes worked together at night. Well, they intended to do so that night. That's all I could get from Carol before she started sobbing like a scared young girl. I put my arm around her to comfort her, then she looked up at me. My God, I will go to my grave never being able to forget the terror behind those eyes."

"Did she say anything else?"

"Yes, she said Terri had been taken and was probably dead." At this point in his story, he looked at me like the next words he would speak would be his last. He was trembling terribly.

"She said that some *thing* killed her. Please understand detective that she was quite mad at this point. I did my best to comfort her but it was, in point of fact, useless. I asked her to tell me exactly what had happened, much like you with me just earlier. So you'll know I can appreciate how you feel. I rushed to the kitchen and offered Carol a glass of cold water, which she cradled like a child and sipped as such. Then she continued on with a tale so fantastic I'd thought she'd lost what sanity she still held onto."

"What did she say?" I must admit that at this point, whether I believed the man in front of me or not, his retelling of the story was much more intoxicating than the lager.

"Carol said they'd been working the *Easy* corner for more than an hour without a single john between them. They were cold and about to call the night, when Terri spots a large hulk of a man lumbering towards them from down the alley. He's walking crooked and erratic and they both figure he's drunk and ripe. They catcalled him, trying to entice him. He didn't respond but loomed closer, growing in size as he neared. Terri continued with her crass dialogue but Carol said she noticed something off about the man, something strange. As he approached, his figure looked wrong, then Carol saw his hands. They drooped abnormally low along the torso and the fingers were gnarled like ancient oak limbs. Then he emerged from the shadowed cloak of the alley and Carol was sure it was she who screamed first."

He stopped here, too afraid to continue. He moved from the wall slightly, as though it was listening to his every word, ready to expose him to whomever or whatever was terrifying him. I, however, needed resolution. Surely this was not where the story ended.

"Then what?"

"I don't know. Carol couldn't finish, she was too distraught. I did manage to help her to her feet and she threw her face into my chest and buried it there for several moments, sobbing painfully. Then she looked up at me and said that she wondered if Terri might still be alive. It was at this point that I contemplated contacting the authorities, but I have a criminal record that involved some robberies and was worried about getting mixed up in a murder investigation."

He could tell by my expression that I wondered about his name and the true extent of his record. I stayed any questioning, allowing him to continue for now.

"I didn't make any calls and said that I'd go have a look, all the while thinking she'd gotten high with Terri and hallucinated something more than a regular john getting too rough with a street girl."

"I would have thought the same," I added, which was a true statement although I said it with the intent to urge him further to the finish.

"As I opened the door, Carol used both hands to slam the door shut and bolted the dead lock. I asked her what was the matter and her reply was that she couldn't go back there, not during the day and certainly not at night. I took her hands in mine and told her it would be okay and that the fiend would be long gone but that we needed to see if Terri was okay and in any need of medical attention. Carol shook her head frantically, telling me that I had no idea what was out there. I tried to reason with her but could not, and told her she could wait in my flat while I went to investigate. Well, the idea of being alone seemed far worse for Carol than returning to the scene in which some apparent grisly act was committed. I of course continued to harbour reservations that anything at all was afoot."

"So you visited the *Easy* corner?" I asked, urging him along.

"I did, and found nothing. All was in order, so much so that when I looked at Carol she had a hardened look of impossibility upon her face. There was not a single splash of blood, in fact the corner itself was immaculately clean and well lit. Carol now looked lost in her thoughts, riddled with confusion. I was now convinced that nothing had happened and the two had been under the influence. It was when I took Carol by the hand to lead her home that I saw it. At first my mind tried to overlook it, lying to itself that the object couldn't possibly be what it was. I crouched down beside the storm drain near the curb. I was in total disbelief. But there, trapped precariously in the ribs of the storm drain was a human ear. I reached down and plucked it free, careful not to let it slide between the steel slots of the drain. It had been severed clean from its victim in what looked like a precise and skilled cut."

The man telling his story looked directly into my eyes, scanning mine to see what I was thinking. Although I found the story interesting, I felt that some sick prank was behind all this. He realized this and shook his head disdainfully.

"I was the same, detective. I believed nothing Carol said, not a word of it. But there it was. A human ear in my hands, as real as the ones on your own head."

"I am sorry, but this is a fairly fantastic story. I've known Carol for a long time and she has been involved with some pretty interesting characters and some even wilder situations."

I relaxed back in my seat and finished the last of my lager. I was ready to leave and figured the guy for a king nut. I dipped into my pocket for my wallet to leave enough for both drinks when the man in front of me threw a clear plastic bag onto the table. The bag contained one unequivocally genuine human ear.

"Shall I finish or does this still no longer interest you, detective?"

I looked down at the small human part, sealed behind a zipped sandwich bag like some piece of jerky. Its pink fleshy colour had long since left and was now only a pale creamy grey.

"What have you done?" I asked, hot with emotion bubbling dangerously close to the surface.

"Not I, detective."

"I don't believe you. You're sick!" There it was, red hot rage burning to come out. I'd seen some things, bad things, but this…

"I wouldn't believe me either, detective. But I can prove it. I know where they both are, where all of them are. Hades couldn't be worse than what I have witnessed!"

He looked sternly at me waiting, to see what I would do. He was right; I didn't believe him but I was sure he believed his own story and if this would lead me to his victims then I needed to play along.

He reached for the bag to put it and its decomposing contents back in his pocket when I grabbed his wrist and took the bag from his hands.

"This is evidence," I said coldly, and slid it into my own pocket. "Why don't you tell the rest of what happened and we'll try to figure this thing out?"

"I'm glad you understand. This whole thing has rattled my nerves so they might never recover."

He looked at me for sympathy but I gave him none. Then he took a sip of his now warm lager, having only barely finished half the bottle and continued.

"As I said, I found the ear resting in the storm drain. I turned and looked at Carol but she wasn't looking at me. She was looking past me, down the alley with horror. I turned to see what had transfixed her. There, at the end of the alley, was a large dark figure, not unlike that of a man but it was hard to tell from such a distance. The light pole was behind the figure, revealing only a dark misshaped silhouette. Then it moved and I knew the first taste of fear that had captivated Carol so intensely. Its movements weren't at all natural but sharp and crooked. Joints bent forcefully, like trying to bend glass without breaking it. My brain told me to run, to grab Carol's arm and run but nothing could move me. The fear was too strong. The next moment the thing was upon me, its terrible grip around my throat. It had eyes, spectral eyes, inside sockets that twitched rapidly with an unimaginable gaze that read the very imprint of your soul."

He stopped and took a long breath as though the thought of his creation would end his miserable life right then.

"Then Carol finally screamed, somehow momentarily free from the fear which imprisoned her, and the thing loosened its grip from my throat. I fell to my knees with my head between them, pleading for air. In the few precious seconds it had taken for me to recover, both Carol and the thing were gone. I got myself to my feet, looked about and found nothing; there was no sign of struggle, not a mark of blood and I was completely sober. Besides the awful knot of fear that lingered within my churning stomach, there was not a single morsel of evidence to be found, that is to say, not a single normal piece of evidence. It is true that I had surveyed for the obvious signs of a kidnapping. But, and I had almost missed it, there was a peculiar growth which had attached itself to the concrete walkway. I crouched down to inspect it and it looked to be a mould; a normal everyday grey mould, not unlike that which would appear on expired cheese, was growing up from the ground. The mould looked as though it stretched on like bread crumbs from those fabled children, urging me to follow. Though I did not want to follow, some foul urge compelled me. The hideous mottled trail of microscopic fungi led me down a series of darkened abandoned streets and alleyways and the farther I went the more I felt the impending danger. After fifteen minutes or so, the mould on the street surface began to grow thick. I took it as a sign that I was getting closer. I had been following so closely in front of my feet that when I looked up, I suddenly stopped. I had come before a large opening that led beneath the city into the sewers. The opening had been grated closed and was covered over heavily with the same grey mould. Two of the steel rib bars had been bent enough to allow me passage, and I did enter."

He stopped here abruptly, as though there was nothing left to tell and that I should be satisfied with this as the ending.

"I expect there's more to be told?" I asked leadingly.

He leaned forward, coming as close as he could to me from across the table, then answered in a barely audible whisper.

"There is, but it cannot be told. It must be witnessed and I will show you, but I warn you detective, your life and nightly slumbers shall never be the same, that is assuming we ourselves survive."

I dismissed his overly dramatic warning. In my head, this was now a simple murder case in which I had spent the better part of the evening sharing a drink with the killer. From here, I was no longer a concerned listener but a Senior Detective of New Scotland Yard with a serious and delicate case to handle. I had considered more than once stopping at my flat for my weapon and a flashlight, but was worried this might spook the man and all would be lost. Therefore, I proceeded into the cool night air with the man, leading me through a maze of streets and alleys. We arrived at the grated opening he had described, and it did seem to be covered in a dense grey mould as he had described. He continued to move hurriedly towards the entrance and I followed, advising we should slow our pace. He was nervous and his eyes revealed a legitimate fear which left me feeling increasingly uneasy.

Only the opening of tunnel was lit by the frail light from the outside street lights. Still, the man proceeded and I followed, doing my best to survey my surroundings as any detective might.

"At the end of the tunnel we go left." He kept walking but turned his head over his shoulder. The light played off the whites of his eyes which caused them to take on an eerie glow.

"Please be prepared as it will become completely black in a few moments. You will need to feel your way along until we reach the lighted portion of the tunnel. Most of the filaments are old and have long since extinguished, but some light will be better than none."

We made our way in complete silence, pressing our hands along the wall like newborns, feeling all sorts of unholy things. Our feet plodded along through a wretched soup which had a fetid stench. Finally, my eyes not quite adjusted to the dark, I was able to register a faint light. The man quickened his pace towards it and I did the same, happy to receive the tiny bit of light given off by the single bulb fastened to the side of the wall. The man stopped, turned and approached me.

"We are close now. Only a few more minutes until we reach the room. I must warn you again detective, what you are about to see will change you."

The terror on his face had momentarily convinced me of everything he'd said and then rational thought replaced my fear. I reassured myself that he was no more dangerous than any other person who has committed a serious crime.

"I am more than prepared to continue," I said, realizing as did he, that my reply was no more than a whisper. As we walked along, I was reminded of something the man had said earlier.

"There is something I need to ask," I started as he continued to walk ahead, as though he hadn't heard me. "Earlier you said Carol and Terri were here, and then you said that they were all here. What did you mean by that?"

Still he continued to walk and said simply, "You'll see soon enough, detective."

My shoes were completely soaked through and my feet now felt pruned inside my socks. My hands likewise were also shrivelled from the dampness. We continued along the labyrinth of tunnels and I took careful note of the many directions we'd travelled to ensure my way back, although I was beginning to lose my confidence that I'd be able to do so. Then the smell hit me in such a way that I staggered momentarily.

I must apologize, as there is no way I could ever hope to explain the stench. The man stopped and signalled for me to do the same. He moved slightly forward as if checking for something, then came back to meet with me.

"We have arrived and from here you must lead. There is no way I could ever enter that room again."

He pointed towards what looked like a large catacomb. The man followed behind me, which was not at all to my liking. I'd be lying if I told you his behaviour had not finally convinced me that this was something far greater than a simple double homicide.

I shuffled forward carefully towards the catacomb. As I approached, a worm of fear slithered up my spine and burrowed deep within me. I looked back at the man who mirrored my own apprehensions. The smell was almost paralysing. The mould was in such abundance that it resembled fur. It was like it was reaching out for me, stretching its hairy mass towards my body as I neared it. It was alive, more so than it should have been. I hunched over, my knees buckling slightly to provide me room to pass unscathed and into the great open room.

At this point, we were slightly elevated, resting atop an eight-foot staircase. If it was possible, the smell had worsened and to my revulsion I discovered why. Beneath the patchwork lighting were the bodies of more than a hundred women. Most were dead and had suffered from what looked like a series of gruesome tortures. A few were still alive, though likely wouldn't last the night. I covered my mouth as the vomit approached my lips but could do nothing to keep it within me.

I wiped my lower lip with my sleeve, unable to even utter a sound.

"You see? I told you, they are all here, every one of them." The man was clutching my arm tightly from fear.

"We need to get out of here and get help, we need to leave immediately."

As I turned to go, the remaining lights hummed loudly and flicked desperately, then expired. Black and nothing more could be seen. The man, who I could no longer see, whimpered softly and I knew he was only a few feet from me.

"Do you smoke?" I asked in a whisper. The man only continued to whimper.

"A light, do you have one?" I repeated urgently.

"N-n-no." His voice was a terrible tremor.

The room was quiet, other than the man beside me who only allowed very faint uncontrollable sounds pass his frightened lips. I too was terrified, trapped atop the tiny staircase, afraid to feel my way out of the room because of the seemingly sentient mould which caked the tomb. I could think of nothing to better our situation. Then I heard it. The man beside me moaned in terror as though he knew a great deal more than I did about its origins. Again came the shuffling of what seemed like heavy feet burdened by a great mass. The movements scratched at the floor and the cries from the still-living audience grew louder. Closer they came, closer still as I stood comatose with fear. I could do nothing and now whatever was moving was close enough that I could hear its body and the unforgettable sounds it made.

I reached for the man beside me and found his arm. "What is it?" I bellowed, "Tell me!"

Yet he was a man drowned in fear and dead from it. My eyes had now fully adjusted to the darkness and yet still saw only black in front of me. I now heard the figure begin to tackle the first step, its joints forcibly bending with a crunch and snap. Suddenly, the lights that had gone out hummed and illuminated the room once more. Now I could see. The man screamed in terror so loud I could not hear even my own. On the step before us was something in the shape of a man but not a man, a thing, a wraith, an awful thing befitting our greatest fears. Its neck bent forward in a terrible hunch and covering its awful body was a large black cloak tied about it like a cape. I managed to gather my wits and prepared to turn when I heard the hideous crack of its upper spine allowing its face to rise and become exposed to me. I could not move. No man should ever know such imagery. The man behind me clung to me tightly as we gaped at the thing before us. Its eyes were far worse then the man had earlier described. There was a goose-like flesh which covered most of its body with the grey mould growing prominently out of tears and openings in the skin. Upon its face it wore what seemed to me a mocking smile but I couldn't be sure.

Then the thing raised its arm and pointed at me. I am sure my heart stopped and I died for a moment on my feet. The man behind me was muttering something incoherent and it momentarily brought me back to my senses. I put my hand on his, which was gripping me painfully and turned my head to look away as the creature navigated the remainder of the stairs. The man was muttering disordered words to me and his eyes bulged from his head.

"What? What is it? What are you saying?"

"The ear, it wants the ear. G-g-give it the ear!"

I turned back to face the thing which now stood towering before me. I reached into my pocket and searched madly for the bag containing the human part. I found it and pulled it free. I shot my hand out madly, clutching the dangling bag in front of my face. The weight of the small object seemed like ten stone and I dropped it in front of me. The thing's eyes turned downward at the fallen bag and its contents, then rose and made contact with mine. I was trembling and felt these were most certainly my final moments. My eyes swirled, jumping from the bodies chained and nailed to the walls, dead or decaying and dying.

The man behind me released my arm. He let escape a shattering scream and ran. I was able to pry myself from my fear and run with all the power my legs possessed down the darkened tunnel behind him. I never looked back as I dashed forward in a mad sprint, following the noise of the man's constant scream which reverberated against the sepulchral walls as though it were a thousand voices at once. I tell you the truth when I say that I was still positive the thing was at my heels and my life was at its end. The rest of my escape was a wash of powerful and terrible emotions as well as numbness; there was a numbness that overcame me and I think that is what saved me that night. I spent the remainder of the evening and early morning hours with both my hands clenched firmly around my service weapon. My heart raced and beat like a firecracker and at certain moments I was confident it might burst. I didn't even dare attempt sleep.

The next day I was early to New Scotland Yard and gathered a large team and took them back to the site, down those darkened tunnels beneath this great city. There was not a single member of the team who were not greatly affected by the discovery of all those bodies and of all those poor tortured women. The creature was nowhere to be found and its presence no longer felt, other than the grim misdeeds which lingered. My partner and long-time colleague disclosed to me that more than half of the women in that awful catacomb were well-known prostitutes. The rest were later identified as the same. The victims had perished due to massive blood loss inflicted by what could only be described as medical incisions running all the way across the abdomen and other parts of the body.

Why? This is a question every good investigator is plagued by on a case from time to time. Although the team combed the streets for leads and suspects, each one rapidly went cold. In my more intimate moments I've developed a theory which borders on mad, especially in the real world where criminals are real people who do really bad things. Still, I'll share with you that I believe there is an evil presence in this world so potent and powerful it is not meant to be witnessed by anyone else but its victims, and may God help those who suffer at its hands and let them know peace.

I am much older now and many years retired as I make this final entry in my journal. As I reflect on past events, there are only four things that remain absolute in my life to this very day: I have never seen the man from that black night ever again, nor have I told a soul the truth about what really happened. I cannot sleep without the aid of prescription pills, and lastly and most importantly, I know with a great and terrible certainty that thing is still out there.

Damned Silverfish

Everywhere,
When the lights go out.
Fast too.

They smile at me like my cocaine friends.
At night you can hear them flitting about,
And talking like a Fitzgerald yarn.

They laugh,
And stand as men stand and lie about as women lie.
They're funny these fish and they know it.
Antennae slicked like Bogey, cracking wise,
Females boasting alloy chests and Dietrich furs.

They make gay and drink gin in crystal,
Chink glasses and spill on the floor.
Bodies rubbing lithely.

More arrive, there's music.
Basie?
Nothing else exists, not tonight.
Not for them,
Not for me.
I'd join them,
I would,
But what to say?

Through a Window Small

A Hooded Warbler perched on the windowsill and gazed into George's backyard. The rain came down in heavy veils and the wind acted as a fresh razor blade against the leaves in the trees. The awning above the window offered a small respite for the fragile bird. His feathers, worn and splintered, his paltry onyx eyes focused with intent. The modest creature stood facing the storm just as a human being would in deep reflection.

George watched the tiny creature from behind the safety of the windowpane and carefully wiped a thin layer of dust from the window with the sleeve of his sweatshirt to get a clear look at the bird. The brilliant lemon colours on the bird's body burned like a miniscule sun in contrast to the muddled sky. The rest of the world seemed to have been fleeced of all colour and existed in an angry state of muted wind and rain.

The bright little creature spread his wings to full extension. He was embracing the storm, challenging its fury and mocking its power. Fearless and ready, the bird left his perch and took flight into the magnificent downpour. George watched as he fought valiantly, then frantically against the ferocious winds. The rain was like a thousand copper pellets against his hollow bones that left him battered against George's backyard fence. He dropped without grace onto the damp earth, succumbing unwillingly to his fate.

George turned and left the kitchen window and made his way to the living room. He plunked back down into his easy chair recliner with a cheese sandwich, which was the reason for his foray into the kitchen some ten minutes earlier. He took the remote control from the seat of his chair and pressed the rewind button. He had missed the important parts during that brief interruption in the backyard.

Things just piled up and time slipped away from everyone

Understanding the Architect

She stood up, then sat down and then stood up again. She paced the smooth, polished tiles and waited for the surgeon to come through the door at the end of the hallway to tell her that her mother was dead. But this part of the story happens on a Monday night, and it is always best to start a day at its beginning.

* * *

The shower drooled warm water onto her head and Kendra realized she hadn't pulled the faucet knob all the way up. She sometimes forgot to do this on the days that she woke up really tired. She gave the knob a firm yank and the faucet head spit water at her three times before a steady even flow rushed forth. She moved her body beneath the water and felt the chill on her skin wash away with the wet heat rushing down around her. This feeling, for a very long time, had been the best part of her day.

She took a towel and wrapped her head, then took another and wrapped it around her chest. She opened the bathroom door an inch or two to let out some of the accumulated steam that was fogging the mirror. She stood and watched as the steam slowly melted away from the small vanity mirror and her worn face appeared in front of her.

"I look a lot older than thirty-three." She didn't actually say the words out loud; she thought them and for a moment stared at her reflection with disbelief.

"It wasn't supposed to be like this," she thought, looking at the thin lines that had formed around her eyes.

Her head fell forward and the wrapped towel came free, allowing dark tendrils of wet hair to dangle in her face. She patted them dry and continued with her morning routine.

She dressed and stood in front of the full-length mirror and inspected herself one final time. The phone rang. She did not want to answer but instinctively moved towards it. She picked up the receiver, cursing herself for doing so. She was already late.

"Hello?"

"Oh, hi Mom. No, I'm just rushing because I'm late for work."

"I haven't heard from him. No, I'm not going to call him. It's over. It was over more than a year ago."

"Sometimes things just stop working, that's what happened. I can't get into this right now, I'm late. How do you feel today?"

"Are you happy to be home?"

"The nurse has been with you all week, right?"

"Good, I'll be by this evening after work."

"Love you too. Bye."

She set the phone back in its cradle and stared blankly into the openness of her apartment. Her mom was sick, really sick, the kind you don't get better from. The last few years had been tough on both of them, what with the diagnosis, then the chemo. They were close, always had been and now her mother was slipping away. In fairness, her relationship with Craig probably would have fallen apart despite her mother's illness but it certainly didn't help matters. Things just piled up and time slipped away from everyone.

* * *

Sometime after 10:00 a.m., she realized she was still idly thinking about the affairs of her life when the phone rang at her desk. She picked it up.

"Oh, hello Sean."

"Your office in five. Okay, talk to you then."

Sean Kelso was her boss's boss. They rarely spoke and it was strange for him to want to see her. She felt a sharp nervous pang ripple through her body. There had been so many layoffs in the last six months and she feared she was next.

She put her phone on call forward, set her email to meeting status and decided to head for the washroom to check her makeup.

She ran the faucets in the washroom until the water was warm and dipped her wrists beneath the soothing water. She looked up at herself in the mirror. Maybe it was nothing. Maybe it had to do with the new project she was heading up. She turned the faucets off, and looked at herself in the mirror one final time. She was going to be let go.

Sean told her it was only temporary, until they finally completed the merger. Then all the company assets would no longer be frozen and in fact, once the merger was completed, loyal employees such as her would most likely receive a pay increase.

The big boys had been saying this for almost two years now while the company slowly sliced away the fat and then trimmed the meat. Now they were picking clean the bone. The economy was tight and the few colleagues she did know who were still working were facing a similar loaded weapon. She would have no choice but to apply for government assistance.

Back at her desk, she sat in her chair and looked around the office at her co-workers. She felt exposed beneath the harsh fluorescent lighting. Every few moments, someone would look up from their computer and make eye contact with her. Did they know already? She felt a sudden urge to leave. She filled her purse with a few personal effects and did not bother to touch her computer or phone. She moved quickly through the reception foyer and out the glass doors. It wasn't until the elevator arrived and the doors opened that she realized she wasn't breathing. The elevator sounded like an Italian church bell when it chimed for the ground floor. She stepped out of the elevator and hastily made for the outside world.

Outside, she felt a small momentary sense of relief. She was suffocating inside the building and only now was able to regulate her breathing and gain some composure. She wanted to cry but didn't. She decided to wait until she got home to let it out, in the safety of her bedroom with the door closed. But she didn't. Rather, she climbed into her comfy bed, pulled the blankets up around her and fell asleep. It wasn't until the phone rang that she woke up.

"Hello?"

"What, no, but I just talked to her this morning."

"Is she okay?"

"What hospital?"

"No, thanks for calling."

She hung up the phone. She knew at that very moment this was it; her mother was going to die.

She sat up on the edge of the bed and looked at the clock. It was already well into the evening; she had slept almost eight hours. She rubbed her eyes, stood up and started to change out of her work clothes and into something more comfortable.

After that she didn't remember much. Her mind was drowning in various thoughts until she realized she was sitting in the waiting room holding a half-empty cup of coffee that she didn't remember buying and didn't remember drinking. She brought the paper rim to her lips, titled the cup and took a sip of the now warm liquid. It was bad coffee, the kind you get from a vending machine in a cup with a little paper handle that you can slip a finger through. She didn't care though about the quality of the coffee. She just needed something to hold onto, something tangible, something to keep her from losing her grip. She was alone in the waiting room. She didn't have any other family other than her mother. She missed Craig a little; he was not very good at much but he knew how to comfort her. Sometimes.

Finally the operating doors opened and a young man came through in full scrubs. He looked weary and she knew the results before he started to speak. Her mother, her Mom, Lily, was dead. After years of fighting and suffering in horrible pain she finally let go. The doctor offered her the opportunity to see her mother and she accepted.

The body had been moved from the battleground of the operating room to another area. The room was empty except for the stretcher on which her mother lay. The light overhead illuminated her mother's features in a way that seemed almost holy. She looked down on her mother's face and reached beneath the surgical blanket to find her hand. It was cold already. The room felt cold too. Her mother looked haggard and worn yet there was still a small presence of peace on her mother's face. She started to sob softly and put her free hand into her mother's hair and leaned in to hold her mother close. She gripped her cold hand as tight as she could and sobbed.

When she left the hospital, the air was cold. The temperature had dropped quite a bit for early fall. She started to cross the street heading towards the hospital parking lot and then stopped before fully crossing. She stood silently for almost ten minutes. There was no traffic, not at this time of night, not on a Monday.

"You son of bitch! How do you think I could ever understand you in all this, this shit! I've lost everything. I've tried my best but I'm not built for this, I can't take much more!" She fell to her knees on the damp street.

"Damn you," she whispered hoarsely, clenching her fist until her knuckles turned bone white.

"You've even taken the hope out of me. I don't want grace when I die, do you hear me? I want a little right now, tonight, this very moment. I need it. Because I want to live, not hold out for something when I die!"

She paused as though she was going to say something else but didn't.

She felt foolish there on her knees in the middle of the street in the dark. She shook her head and let out a short hoarse laugh, then stood up. She looked up into the night sky like so many fools had done before her, searching for something that couldn't be seen. She didn't find anything but she couldn't quit looking.

She got in her car and drove home. She climbed up the stairs to her bedroom, did not undress, fell on her bed and slept for twenty-three hours.

Two weeks later she received a phone call from her employer advising her that the merger was completed and they were delighted to invite her back to work with an embarrassingly modest pay increase. She accepted. Her life at work was better with the pressure of upper management drama now gone and she delved in to reprise her role with the company.

At night though, when she was alone, she cried a lot. She cried over various things in her life but mostly she just felt a terrible void all the time. She had no purpose and moved through each day robotically. Every day was a routine for her. It needed to be as such to maintain order in her life.

Two years later, she was leaving the grocery store and her items came out of the bottom of her bag. Nothing broke but her fruit scattered all over the pavement, her oranges rolling away like escaped convicts with freedom in sight. A man stooped to help her gather her items and even walked her to her car. He said his name was Michael. They married almost three years later in Mexico.

On her thirty-eighth birthday she developed flu-like symptoms that lasted almost a week and decided to see her doctor. The doctor advised that she was pregnant. When she was with Craig and trying to conceive, a doctor had told her that she was not able to bear children. This was only one of many reasons that culminated in their split.

"How is this possible? I was told I couldn't have children."

"Well, that may have been the case then but right now you are most certainly pregnant."

"I am?"

"You are. Congratulations Mrs. Dodd."

Lily Elaine Dodd was born on a hot July afternoon. As the doctor handed over the newborn child, she took her daughter into her arms and held her baby cheek to cheek. She felt a little bit of hope once again.

The Mustang

Skating in heat upon plain
Haunches full
The last runs and final breadth
With final breath

Hooves pound out thunder
Soil tears betwixt each beat
Not for distance
Not for stride
Nor pride
But borne of will
And of freedom
Because he can
Then gone forever

Plastic Query

THE PHONE RANG TWICE AND then someone picked up.

"Argenti Manufacturers." The voice was soft and somewhat effeminate. It was impossible to accurately determine the person's sex.

Wendell suddenly felt foolish and asked, "Have I reached the ordering department?"

"Yes Sir, you have. May I have your store ID and PST number?"

Wendell fumbled through some papers on his desk and quietly cursed underneath his moustache for being so disorganized.

"Sorry for the wait," he said, adjusting his glasses so they perched correctly on the bridge of his nose. "The ID is 35862ARP and the PST number is 334560999002."

"Thank you sir, and how may I help you today?"

"Um, well, I need to order some mannequins."

"Yes sir of course, we only sell mannequins."

"Ah, right." Wendell felt lost and the person on the other end of line tried to help by continuing to probe with questions.

"How many do you need sir?"

"Um, I would say six would do fine."

"Female or male?"

"All female, it's a women's store."

"With nipples or without?"

"Excuse me?"

"Do you want the female mannequins to have nipples or not to have nipples?"

"Don't all women have nipples?"

"Real women surely do sir, but with our mannequins you have the choice." Wendell slumped back in his chair and rubbed his fingertips across his perspiring brow.

"I see, well, I'm not sure. Why do you make them two different ways?"

"It depends on how you want your display to look. A mannequin with nipples will create the illusion of firm nipples beneath the garment whereas the mannequin without nipples will not. The mannequins with nipples have a more obvious erotic feature to them. It depends on what you're looking for."

Wendell swallowed hard and wondered if the person on the other end could hear. "I guess I'll order the mannequins with nipples. It seems more natural, doesn't it?"

"I think so sir."

"Okay, then let's do that."

"Do you want full bodies or just torsos?"

"Full bodies. They'll be wearing pants so I'll need full bodies."

"Fine, sir. Now how about colour?"

"Colour?"

"Yes of course, we have all the most popular ethnicities."

"White. All white," he felt he answered too quickly. He realized he had no idea who the person was on the other end of the line. Wendell wasn't even sure if the person was male or female. "Maybe one bla… ah, African American and five whites."

"That's fine sir, however the Asian mannequins are quite popular."

Wendell felt defeated for some reason. "Okay, fine, make it four whites, one African American and one Asian."

"Very good, sir. I've entered the order and it should ship in about five business days."

"Alright, thank you."

"My pleasure sir, have a wonderful day."

Wendell held the receiver to his ear for a few moments longer, then hung up as well. He leafed through some papers on his desk and found the phone number for his next call. He read the company name on the business card between his thumb and forefinger and somehow felt this call would be worse.

Elementary Weather

On my stomach
The clouds are cotton above me
Floating stationary
Soft and supple

Temperature drops by two
Cotton daubed grey
Crusty and firm
Blue elliptical cut-outs in haphazard sizes
Fall in great numbers
Thousands of cocktail umbrellas open

Angry yellow pipe cleaners
Bend and thrust from beneath the cotton
They deck the sky with fury
Electric upon my skin
Chill in my bones

Then the glue weakens
The cotton falls and disappears
Reveals a bright yellow painted circle
A perimeter of orange clay spikes

On my back
I watch
I warm
Two plastic eyes open
The black centres shake foolishly
A row of elbow noodle teeth smile down upon me

Charleswood Road

"There's no way you'll eat that," I said.

"Oh really? How much you want to bet?"

"A Mac Meal. I'll bet a Mac Meal you won't eat that."

I met Damian in the halls of Oak Park High. I was in my senior year and Damian was two years my junior. We had been introduced by Bill Boudreaux who was in the same grade as I was. Damian was the same age as my younger brother Ryan and they had classes together.

I subsequently lost the bet to Damian who proceeded to eat the entire earthworm off the side of the road and then enjoyed a greasy burger and fries courtesy of my emaciated pocketbook. Damian was a skater, rather I should say he skateboarded and was better at it than anyone I had seen skate in school. Bill skated too and I had met him at the Edge skate park only a few weeks prior. It was Bill and Damian who introduced Ryan and me to the other skaters who attended our high school.

Oak Park High was located in a south-end suburb of Winnipeg at the corner of Charleswood Road and Rannock Avenue. I had moved from Regina to Winnipeg with my family. While our new house was being renovated, we lived downtown on Hargrave Street in this crappy apartment complex called the Howard Towers.

My family moved around a lot. My father would move us from one place to another because of work. We eventually moved into a southwest Winnipeg subdivision, which made the bus commute to school much easier.

Ryan and I attended Oak Park High together. Each morning we had to catch the 66 Grant bus from downtown and bulldoze into the suburbs. We had moved five times in eleven years and although each time became harder than the last, my brother and I were now masters at starting over. We had become accustomed to the subtle nuances of the hormonal jungle known as high school. We also understood that gaining peer acceptance was a skilled art and that having an angle was a big help.

Skating was that angle. It was the first day of our second week attending

Oak Park High and the noon bell had just gone off. I searched my disastrous locker for my lunch bag. Ryan had his locker beside mine. We had arrived a few weeks into first semester so the Vice Principal found us two unused lockers side by side. Ryan stood waiting with his lunch already in hand. Bill came by our lockers to meet up and we headed down to the cafeteria together. When we sat down, Damian went around the lunch table and introduced the others. There was Ash, whom I'd already seen around school. He had a brother the same age as Bill and I but we didn't hang out with him much. Todd Johnson reached across the table to formally shake my brother's hand and mine and then asked if we wanted to trade our Dunk-a-Roos for his butterscotch pudding. We both declined.

We had ourselves a regular high school clique except we had no interest in being cool or popular. The truth was we weren't popular; in fact we were more social outcasts than anything else. Our peers couldn't connect with us because we went against the grain in the way we dressed and the music we listened to. Our interests were eclectic and strange. None of us played football, which was the promoted sport at Oak Park High. Our teachers didn't know what to make of us; they could barely understand us with all the skate jargon we used. We only wanted to skate and joke and prank and skate some more. And then eat.

Skating consumed us, so much so that we were almost perpetually late for class each morning and after lunch. We had set up grind boxes and low rails in the side parking lot, much to the faculty's disapproval because that was the teachers' parking lot. Todd Johnson, Ash and I would bring thick wool socks to school and slip them over our regular socks during lunch so that we could slide down the wooden handrails on our shoeless feet. The wool socks made the rails so much easier to slide and by the time you reached the end of the twelve-stair flight, you were really cooking.

Ash was a good skater who was also even better on a snowboard, despite living in the one of the flattest cities in the world. Todd was a born ladies man and was the only one of our friends who ever managed to keep a steady girlfriend. He dated this bird named Andria and they fought like feral cats most days, but we all envied him for having a female around all the time.

I had very little interest in school studies. It's too bad really, as I was a voracious reader of all genres and had a keen interest in music and the arts. I loved to draw and paint, but I loathed school, homework, exams and that sort of crap. I was also a lover of comic books and during final period I would sit and watch the second hand rotate on the classroom clock, doodling superheroes in the margins of my writing assignments. When the bell rang I talked to no one. I would make my way to my locker where Ryan was waiting for me. We would gather up a few books to make it look like we had homework to do and race towards the bus stop.

We always tried to sit in the back of the bus, because that's what kids in high school do. My brother had met a kid in one of his classes who introduced himself as the Beave. Everyone else called him the Beave as well and I suspected the Beave might be cool because he carried a skateboard under his arm. Both my brother and I were also skaters, although we rode inline skates instead. The Beave took the bus downtown with us almost every day even though he didn't live downtown. To this day I still don't know where the Beave actually lived. One afternoon as we pulled away from the school, the Beave pointed back towards the school's entrance.

"Lookee!" His nose twitched like a rodent's.

The Beave was pointing at the school's sign, which was a series of individual letters mounted high above the front entrance doors. Someone had climbed the roof and painted in the letter "T" in front the word Oak.

"Haha, Toak Park. Get it? Man I bet Jimmy the Banger put that up there. He's a genius. That dude loves to blaze."

The Beave rotated himself in his seat to face us.

"Check this out. I boosted it from Chem class today."

The Beave had a tin cigarette container in his hand. He opened the lid and inside was a viscous shiny silver liquid.

"That looks like mercury," I blurted, not able to curb the shock in my voice.

"It is mercury," said the Beave with a mischievous smile which formed seemingly in slow motion across his face.

The bus came to a stop unexpectedly and the Beave lost his grip on the cigarette box. It tumbled to the ground, hit the floor and the quicksilver lived up to its name, running chaotically between the vinyl grooves of the flooring of the bus. The Beave lifted his feet off the floor and crossed his legs on the seat. My brother and I followed his lead. We watched, mesmerized, as beads of mercury raced against themselves, back and forth with each movement of the bus, like an ocean's tide.

At our stop downtown, the Beave exited with us. We told him we were heading to our place to grab a snack and our skates then we were going to head over to the Edge to ride the ramps.

"The Edge, yeah, I skate there all the time," he said looking over his shoulder, completely disinterested.

"Do you want to come with?" I asked.

"Nah, I got some business downtown," he shrugged and started off on his own.

My brother and I skated the Edge almost everyday for five years and we never saw the Beave there once.

* * *

The Edge Skate Park was originally located on Nairn Street in an old fire station. They had a four-foot mini ramp with a six-foot extension on one side. There were some scattered quarter pipes and various street obstacles, but the real draw was the eleven-foot vert half pipe with a roll in. The ramp was so high you could catch air between the steel columns of the rafters. The masonite surface had been painted with black paint that made it twice as slick. A few years back, this skater named Dennis took a bucket of grimy water and added three cans of cola to it. Then he mopped the whole surface of the ramp and let it dry. The sugar from the cola-water mixture gave our urethane wheels the perfect traction. From then on, someone mopped the floor the same way before every session.

The skate park had opened its doors in 1989 and two guys named Peter and Luke ran the skate sessions. Over the course of a year, the youth patronage grew exponentially until an announcement was made during a session that the Edge would close its doors and re-open in a new location at the corner of Lily and Pacific Avenue in the heart of Winnipeg's exchange district.

Luke opted not to reprise his role of running the new Edge location, while Peter was ecstatic about the new spot. Peter handled the design and layout of the skate park ramps and street course, all the while listening intently to the requests from the various skaters who anxiously awaited the doors to open. Damian, Ash, Ryan and I even answered the call for volunteers because it meant we could skate for free anytime we wanted to. We also liked Peter.

Peter was cool. Besides being able to "talk the talk" about skating or biking, he also knew a lot about other street things such as graffiti art. He was a graph master and he used the walls of the new Edge as his canvas. I connected with him because of my own personal interest in art and drawing. Meanwhile at school, my grades began to slip more and more. The only class I participated in was art class, which is where I met Terry. He was two years older than me but hadn't graduated yet.

"Art doesn't have deadlines," he would say. "I have a very stringent process of elimination. If it doesn't feel right than it isn't."

It seemed to me that he never finished any art piece he started. Terry never really worked all that hard at his artwork but stressed about it all the time. This was oddly uncharacteristic of him though, because outside of art class he had a very simple and laid back approach to everything. A lot of girls liked Terry because he was so easygoing but more importantly because he was old enough to buy them booze whenever there was a party.

Terry liked to drink himself. His choice was always beer and it was rare to see him without a beer in his hand, although he never appeared to be drunk. He didn't slur his words or stumble around. He was sharp, quick-witted and even occasionally charming.

Terry also held two jobs, which came as a surprise to me, probably due to his lackadaisical attitude. He worked at the drive-in movie theatre and gave free admission to my broke friends and me because he worked the ticket wicket. I liked Terry. Not because he let us in for free but because he didn't do it to gain favour, he just did it, even though Damian and Todd were dressed only in their boxer shorts at the time because of the intense summer heat.

Terry also held a job at a local convenience store in Charleswood. He worked at the store on weekends and the theatre most other nights. Some of my other friends like Bill and Damian worked jobs but eventually got fired for being late, eating the merchandise, being rude to customers, or whatever teenage delinquent act seemed appropriate that day.

School rolled on and into the second semester. It was going to be a difficult second term with a tough load of classes, which included math and chemistry. I didn't know anyone in my chemistry class. The lab desks sat two at a table. When I arrived, I sat alone in the back with the intention not be noticed. My plan lasted all of fifty-eight seconds.

"This seat taken?"

Her name was Dana and I'd seen her hanging around the smokers' doors even though she didn't smoke. She hung out with kids your parents wouldn't want you to hang out with and in this instance, your parents would be right for once. She had long dark hair and small lips and didn't dress like the other girls. She dressed kind of like a punk and kind of like a folkie. She always wore dark boots with flat heels cut just below the knee, which made her look taller than she was. She wasn't fat or thin but landed somewhere in the middle. She looked good and she knew it. She often got her way with people, especially guys.

"It's a yes or no," she said, waiting for me to stop staring.

"No."

"Good. I hate sitting in the front."

I smiled. "Me too, I always sit in the back. I do the same on the bus."

"You take the bus?"

"Yeah, I live downtown. But we're moving soon."

She made intense eye contact with me. I felt uncomfortable but didn't look away.

"You're not from Winnipeg?"

"No, we moved here from Regina not too long ago."

"A new-boy."

"I guess, whatever that is."

"It's a boy who is new. It's not supernatural. You sure you're ready for chemistry class?" she mocked, smiling at me.

I screwed my face up a little at her. "It was this or biology. I kind of wish I'd selected biology."

"Yeah I know. Then you wouldn't have to sit beside me. I talk a lot."

"No it's not you it's—" She cut me off.

"I know it's not me." She smiled in a nonchalant way looking down at her class schedule then looked back up at me. The room got warm.

I saw a lot of Dana over the next few weeks. She always seemed to pop up wherever I was. My feelings about her were complicated; she was attractive, an opinion that was shared by many, but something about her made me only want to be her friend and nothing more. Other high school girls worried about candy coloured lip-gloss, the brand of jeans they wore and who would date Rodney, the Captain of the Raiders. Dana didn't give a shit and I liked that a lot.

* * *

As summer rapidly approached so did the last days of school. We had finally moved into our new home. When living in Regina, my brother and I had an eight-foot half pipe in our back yard. My father, who had promised our move to Winnipeg was the last one we'd make, had hard time convincing us of such. As part of his bargaining posture, he offered an amount of cash to build a new eleven-foot half pipe in our back yard once we had settled in.

In art class, I mentioned to Terry that I was building a half pipe in my back yard because at some point, he had mentioned that he used to skateboard. Terry said he had actually built many ramps in the past for friends.

"You don't believe me?" he asked, sensing my lack of faith in his completion skills.

"It's not that I don't believe you, it's just, well, you're so busy here," I said, trying to change the slant of my words by emphasizing how important his art was.

"The art can wait. The summer's here my friend, a ramp waits for no man. We must build this thing and then we must skate it." He looked crazed, but his enthusiasm was genuine and hard to ignore.

My dad was thrilled that Terry was going to help build the ramp because Terry agreed to work for beer. As long as my dad had beer waiting for him, Terry showed up for work, and on time too. We would work on the ramp and then go street skating together. Sometimes Damian or Ash would join us, who were more than anxious to see the ramp completed. In the meantime, we divided our time between skating the Edge and skating the street. We spent the greater part of our summer driving around in my parent's minivan, scoping out spots to skate around the city of Winnipeg.

Skating on the street happened mostly later at night because the local businesses didn't like you skating on their property and often if a business employed a security guard, they would yell at us to leave the premises. This of course was understandable, however we selected our responses very carefully and tried our best to articulate a strong curse word into an intelligent sentence. Damian once pulled down his jeans and the city of Winnipeg experienced two full moons in one evening. There was the odd time that we would be approached by a real police officer. We spoke less abrasively towards the police but still showed little to no respect for them. We weren't bad kids really; we just didn't understand all the forced discipline and authoritative bull being jammed down our throats. Thus we often responded to people in negative ways. In truth we just wanted to skate which to us seemed like a very wholesome activity, despite the late hours we did it at. When most other kids were trying to score alcohol illegally or were hot-boxing their cars and smoking up with their friends, we were out sliding down handrails, trying our best to get good at something that unfortunately no one else understood except us.

Terry and I continued to work on the ramp. We wanted to finish it before school ended so we could start skating it immediately. We did run into some snags though.

"I'm not sure that's right," I said, looking at one of the braces supporting the lower transition on the ramp.

"If it doesn't feel right than it isn't." Terry was looking at the crude spec drawing he had made during art class.

Terry put back the rest of his beer and popped the cap on a fresh one.

"No big deal. Let's go skate a bit and clear our heads. Things will look right when we get back."

I didn't see how avoiding the problem was going to fix it but Terry seemed pretty persuasive. I agreed to take a break as we had been working almost all evening and it was starting to get dark. When we got back, the sun had disappeared completely and the sky was black.

"See? Problem solved," he said, looking at the ramp.

I looked too, but it was too dark to see the problem anymore. Terry seemed satisfied with these results and grabbed another beer.

* * *

It was Friday and chemistry class was almost over. I had a hard time staying awake and kept nodding off, but Dana kept jabbing me in the side with her elbow to wake me up. I looked up at the clock and did my best to stay awake for the last twenty minutes of class. Dana handed me a tiny little book she had made during class, which consisted of an encyclopaedia of skater slang words. It was actually rather impressive and had little explanatory drawings to accompany certain words. The booklet had an elastic binding and I spent the remainder of class rather entertained.

When the bell rang, I collected my books and started to make for the door.

"Where are you off to so fast?" Dana asked pryingly.

"Nowhere. It's Friday and I want to get out of this place."

Dana looked at me and said nothing for a moment.

"Oh, okay." She looked disappointed.

"What's up?"

"Nothing, I was just going to ask if you wanted to go to a party with me and a couple of my friends tonight, but if you're hanging out with your gang…" She said the last part with a sarcastic eye roll.

"Nope, I was just going to work on the ramp with Terry but I could do something after that. Besides, we can only work outside until it gets dark."

"Cool, I have my parent's car tonight. I'll pick you up at nine?"

"Yeah, okay, sure."

She wore a sincere smile when I accepted. I suddenly felt nervous. I had never met any of her friends. They didn't even go to our school.

I met Damian and Ash in the hallway outside of chemistry class and we walked to my locker. Todd was there with Bill and my brother. They had all made plans to go street skating downtown that evening.

"You and Ryan going to take the van and meet us there?" asked Damian.

"I can't guys, I've got plans with Dana."

Damian laughed. "Ouch! You're gonna ditch us for a bird?"

"Come on man, it's not like that at all, plus she's not that bad," I said defensively.

"I heard she hangs with some pretty messed up dudes down on Osborne on the weekends," added Ash, looking genuinely concerned.

I had never thought to ask Dana where the party was. I had also heard the rumours about her too but never cared.

Todd was smiling at me then looked at the rest of the gang, "You all have got to cool down. Your boy here is heading out with a girl tonight. When is the last time any of you went out with a girl?" If there had been any crickets in the walls of Oak Park High they had missed their cue that afternoon.

That evening, Terry sat on the curb of my driveway and sipped a cold beer as the sun fell over the western horizon. I sat next to him and had just popped the top on a can of cola. I set the can out in front of me on the road.

"You popped it but aren't drinking it. That's a crime in some countries, you know," said Terry, looking down at the perspiring can in the warm summer heat.

"I like to let it breathe a bit," I said, half smiling. "You think we'll finish the ramp before school's out for summer?" I asked.

"Yup, well maybe, I don't know. We'll finish when we finish." It was a classic Terry answer. I took a sip of cola. The smudgy colours of the setting sun had been painted across the sky. We sat and drank until a Plymouth Reliant pulled into my driveway. Dana killed the headlights and stepped out of the car.

"Hey Terry."

"Hey Dana."

"You two know each other?"

"Yup." They both answered exactly the same way at the exact same time.

"You ready to go?" Dana asked, looking past Terry to me.

"Yeah sure," I replied, and then looked at Terry. "You want to work on the ramp tomorrow or something?"

"Maybe, if your dad fills the beer fridge. He's all out." Terry got up and walked down the street, waving with his back to us.

Dana was leaning up against the passenger door. She looked the same as always; I was surprised that she wasn't more dressed up for the party. She opened the door for me and went around to the driver's side. She got in and started the car. The cassette player was on and the Descendants came through the speakers.

"I know it's not the Ramones but this will have to do," she joked. She knew the Ramones were one of my favourite bands.

"I like the Descendants too," I said, trying to stand up for my musical tastes. "How do you know Terry?" I tried changing the subject.

Dana smiled, acknowledging my ploy. "Everyone knows Terry. He bought me beer a couple of times"

I should've known.

We picked up Dana's two friends Janie and Kara. Both girls were rather made up and wore provocative clothes which accentuated certain key areas of their form. In all honesty, I was uncomfortable. If it had been Todd, he would've been right at home in situation like this but I tried my best to hide my nerves.

I felt out of place at the party too. I didn't know anyone and Dana disappeared for a while, leaving me to fend for myself amongst the drunken fodder. I met a guy who said he used to skate when he was younger. He looked really old because he had grey coming through the stubble on his face. He seemed nice enough so I did my best to cling to him for a while and pretend to be interested in the topics he wanted to discuss, such as why two and two shouldn't make four and the notion that the perfect joint is not made but rather is a state of consciousness. I was out of my league.

Dana eventually found me and seemed to have misplaced certain articles of her clothing. She was also drunk but still somewhat coherent. I told her I was going to check out because I was bored and offered to drive her home. She declined and I asked how she intended to get home. She said she was close with the owner of the place and always stayed over on a party night.

"You gonna be able to find your way home, new-boy?"

"Yeah, the guys are downtown skating anyway. I know the spots, I'll find them or take the bus."

Dana swayed a bit like she was going to topple over. I caught her and straightened her out.

"Nice save, new-boy." She looked down at my hands which were holding her arms. She looked up at me. Her face was flushed with red and her eyes were under the influence. I took my hands away.

"Had enough, have you?"

"I…"

"You what?"

"I'm going to take off." I didn't like her like this. She was too aggressive. I made my way through the confined sweaty bodies, broken beer bottles, clouds of smoke and even a few passed out dogs in search of the door. As I left, I could hear Dana faintly in the background behind me.

"Bye, new-boy."

I eventually did find the gang skating a set of stairs at a building downtown. It's not hard to locate skaters in the city of Winnipeg at night if you know where to look. Damian and Ash were trying to kick flip down a set of stairs at least eight steps wide. I saw my brother sitting on the far side of the steps with Bill and Todd.

"Well, if it isn't Casanova," yelled Bill into the silent air as I came into sight.

I smiled, "Not likely."

I took a seat next to my brother.

"They land it yet?" I asked the three onlookers as Ash stumbled on the landing and his skateboard shot away in front of him. Ash silently got right back up on his feet, dusted himself off, fetched his board and climbed back up the steps to try again.

"Nah, they just started to hit this thing," said Bill.

Todd looked past Bill at me. "Where's Dana?"

"Back at the party. I guess. It was lame and I was really bored."

Todd smiled. "Girls!"

I sure didn't understand girls. It was like everything they did or said was a big mystery. Half the time they just looked at you like they could read your mind and eventually would made some sort of facial gesture, but then said nothing. The worst part wasn't the cryptic things they said but the things they held back and didn't say.

My brother changed the subject and informed me that they had gone to the Edge to skate earlier. Peter had mentioned that we could skate a private session tomorrow because he had a few repairs to do around the park. That cheered me up and I went to go grab my skates from the trunk of their van. As I started to walk away, Damian landed a kick flip clean down the stairwell and almost rode right into me.

"Hey buddy," he said and slapped me five.

"Nice catch," I said, congratulating him on the landed trick.

"No biggie. Watch Ash 'cause he's about to board-flip down the set."

Ash rolled up and landed a board-flip just as Damian had called it. Only a few moments later, a security guard appeared at the top of the stairs and advised that we had to leave as the police had been informed of our presence. The guy was nice about it and no one gave him any grief as we packed it in.

We piled into the van and went to a few other spots, then hit a drive-thru for some food. We also added about ten cups of water to our order. We drove around in the van with the sliding back door open, providing drive-by cool downs to unsuspecting people on the sidewalk. Some were pleased, some weren't. We felt it was our civic duty to continue until all the cups were empty. Then we headed for home.

* * *

I took a seat on the bench and watched as Damian tried in vain to feeble grind along the quarter pipe. Peter took a seat beside me and handed me a can of cold soda.

"That kid is getting good!" He popped the tab on the can and it made gurgling sound. "So are you," he added.

I looked over at him. No adult had ever said anything about my skating before, let alone something in the way of a compliment. I didn't know what to say.

"I've heard around that someone from Maverick Skates is interested in talking to you. That true?"

"Yeah, there was a rep here last week watching me skate. I guess they need some skaters to do shows and demos overseas. He said there'll be some professional contests they'll be entering me in also."

"What do you think of all that?"

I told him I was really interested in traveling and getting paid to do something I loved.

"I bet it would be pretty sweet to see new places and meet new people all because of skating," he offered.

I smiled. I had the feeling Peter was worried about me still being in high school and taking off alone around the world. Damian landing the feeble grind interrupted my thoughts. He rolled over on his board and took a seat beside Peter and me.

"You see that shit?" he asked, breathing heavily.

"I did, but you could've come out fakie, it would've looked cooler."

I promptly received a punch in the arm for my joke and Damian rolled away. Bill, Todd and my brother were sitting up on the landing of the spine ramp while Ash skated in the transition.

"You guys want to go grab some wings after this?" asked Peter as he watched Damian roll by. "It's on me."

"I don't think that will be a hard sell," I replied.

At the restaurant, Damian crowded into the booth next to me, Ash, and Todd even though there was more room on the other side with Bill, Peter and Ryan. Ash took some water into the straw of his beverage and spit it down Damian's back. He wreathed and wriggled uncomfortably from the cold wet feeling running down his back and changed to the other side of the booth accordingly.

Peter took us out now and again for food. He didn't have kids of his own, so I think this was his way of being a bit of a dad. He always gave us all a ride back to one of our houses which meant we didn't have to take the bus. But these kind gestures weren't what made Peter cool; he listened to us in a way most adults didn't. He also understood the things we were into because he used to be into them too and still messed around on a skateboard from time to time. He built and maintained all the ramps in the park, so we could always talk about the possibility of a new obstacle. He even introduced us all to a great band called the Undertones.

Bill and Todd ordered "super hot" wings and had to eat two bowls of vanilla ice cream afterwards because their stomachs were on fire. Ash mixed six different table condiments together, including vinegar, ketchup, mustard, soya sauce, hot sauce and three packets of sugar. He then dared Damian to drink the concoction. Despite having eaten two pounds of wings and fries, Damian asked for his usual payment of a Mac Meal. Ash agreed to the terms and Damian put the hideous liquid down his throat. He promptly vomited on the floor beside the booth. Peter signalled for the cheque.

*   *   *

On Sunday, Terry came by my house to work on the ramp. My father had restocked the beer and we set out to complete the final stages of the work. We worked beneath the hot sun until the damn thing decided to leave us. We had put in a full day of work and now stood back and looked upon the completed ramp. We just stood there and stared for who knows how long. It was Terry who broke the silence.

"This feels right."

I smiled. It was his finest piece of art work and the only thing he ever finished. That night Terry had to work at the convenience store. Two men with guns robbed the store. Terry ran out after them to get the license plate number and a third person, the lookout, shot him in the face with a shotgun. He died two days later in the hospital.

I didn't go to school on Monday. I told my parents I was sick. I think they knew the truth though. I spent most of the day in bed. When I finally got up I went to the window of the backyard and looked out at the lonely ramp. It was beautiful day, perfect. He never even got to ride it once. They say time heals all wounds; I've never stopped thinking of Terry though and it hurts to this day every time I do.

* * *

It was two weeks into summer vacation and the gang had spent almost every day in my parents' backyard skating the ramp. My friends never mentioned Terry or the events surrounding his death and I was grateful for it. I had attended his funeral just before school ended. I went with Dana. She was quiet and not at all herself. In fact, she didn't really say anything to me and left without saying goodbye. That evening when I called, her parents answered and said she wasn't feeling well. I asked if I could speak to her anyway. They called out to her and Dana answered the phone.

"Hello, new-boy. What do you want?"

"You're not sick, are you?"

There was pause. "No, not the kind you're thinking of."

She wasn't responding sarcastically like she usually did; she sounded meek but serious.

"What's wrong?" I asked, concerned.

"Nothing."

I pried a little harder. "Is it about Terry?"

"Why don't you mind your own fucking business!" She slammed the receiver down and hung up.

I listened to the dial tone in shock, and then I finally hung up the phone too.

A few weeks passed and I concentrated on skating the ramp in my backyard. I had been trying to learn how to do a McTwist and couldn't quite stick the landing. I skated well into the evening and my parents flicked on the backyard light for me. I stood on the landing at the top of the ramp. I was eleven feet up and over the roof of my parent's bungalow I could see a car pull into the driveway. Dana stepped out and waved at me. She came around back and I skated down the ramp to meet her.

Dana sat in the chair next to me as I proceeded to take off my skates, pretending to do some adjustments to my bindings.

"I'm pregnant."

I dropped my skate. I looked at her.

"It happened at the party, after you left. I was really drunk and tried to sleep it off and a guy came into the room and…and…I, he held me down and I was so drunk I couldn't stop him."

She started to sob. I didn't know what to say. I just put my arm around her while she cried.

After a while she stopped and looked up at me. Her eyes were puffy and her face was blotchy.

"I don't really remember it that much, you know. I tried to stop him, I told him to stop and then I must have passed out."

I still couldn't find any words; my tongue felt dry and my throat was raw and parched.

"I'm sorry," I said finally.

"I'm sorry too. I mean for yelling at you." She paused again, working her way up to say something else.

"Will you go to the doctor with me? I'm really scared."

"Right now?"

"No, yeah, I guess. I don't think I can do it alone."

"What about your parents? Have you told them anything?"

"No." She looked away from me and I could tell she felt filled with shame.

"Okay, I'll go with you. I'll do it."

She looked back at me and didn't say anything. She didn't have to. The look on her face made her thoughts clear.

I read a magazine about hunting in the waiting room. I found it weird that a hospital would have a magazine about killing in a place that was supposed to save lives. After about three hours of waiting I got up to go to the vending machine to buy a beverage. I took a sip and set the can on top of the machine. I reached over my head to stretch and a powerful yawn pushed free. My weary arms found their place again at my side and as they settled, I felt a tap on my shoulder. I turned and Dana was there. Her face looked worn and pale, her eyes expressed an exaggerated fatigue.

"Let's go." That was all she said.

I was so anxious to know what had happened that I left the soda can on top of the vending machine.

In the car Dana said nothing so I in turn said nothing, waiting patiently for her to talk. Only she wasn't going to say anything; I could tell. I wanted to ask her what the doctor had said but was afraid she would get angry with me for prying into her privacy again. Like a fool I did it anyway.

"You okay?"

There was a long silence before she responded.

"The doctor said I had a miscarriage. You see, I wasn't lying when you called the other night and I said I was sick but not how you think. I was sick. There was a lot of blood I was so scared. I yelled at you but I really wanted to tell you the truth right then. I should have gone to see the doctor right away but couldn't face my parents."

There were tears coming down her cheeks but she didn't realize she was crying. I put my hand on her hand. She looked over at me and then back on the road. She didn't say anything else and neither did I.

* * *

By mid-summer, I had signed a contract with Maverick Skates for a year to skate in contests and shows in various countries, starting in China. I met Peter for lunch as he had known the news even before I did. Peter and I ate lunch and talked like real friends do. After lunch, I felt it right to shake Peter's hand for all he had done for my friends and me over the last year. He shook his head at my hand.

"I think good friends can do better." And we hugged.

That was the last time I ever saw Peter. He would die from a heart attack while I was only a month into my first world tour. I missed his funeral.

I visited Dana at her house the night I signed the contract. I told her my news and that I would be leaving before the end of the summer. She told me she was also leaving at the end of the summer as she'd been accepted to attend UBC. We didn't say much after we exposed our respective new life paths. Everything was changing so fast all of a sudden.

"My friends are having a going away party for me next week," she said, looking down at the ground. "Will you come?"

"Yeah, sure, of course."

She smiled a little. "I'm going to go inside. Maybe I'll see you tomorrow?"

I walked home and tried my best not to think about all the things that had happened during my final high school summer. I reached down on the ground and picked up some flat stones and threw them one by one into the puddles on the side of the road as I walked. For a moment, I wished it were two years ago when all I had to do was get passing grades in school and skate for kicks. Now everything felt so...adult. I could feel that the weight and complexities of life were more than I could understand or handle. I found it hard to find answers to why bad things happen to good people like Terry or Dana. Maybe there were no answers and things just happened. Maybe we are just supposed to cope with them the best we know how. It was a bitter resolution but the only one I could find on a walk home.

*   *   *

At night, the gang and I street-skated a lot. Their reaction to the news about me going away to skate was good. Bill and Todd bickered about the best concrete ledge to skate overseas. They did however agree that the concrete bowl in Marseille was the best in the world. France was somewhere in the middle of the tour and promised I would skate it as much as possible.

Ash gave me a hug and made me swear to send him a post card from each country I was in. Damian was surprisingly quiet about the whole thing. When we drove home that night in the van I was in the far back bench with him and he leaned in to talk to me.

"You gonna skate the bowl in Munster?" he asked quietly.

"Yup," I replied

"Good. What about London? There's that ledge on London Bridge, I mean, you gotta grind that right?"

"I will."

"Okay, good."

He reached his hand out for mine and he shook it like regular folks did; there was no high five. He just took my hand and shook it like we had made deal, and that was that.

We skated a lot those final nights and made noise, ate bad food and drank Slurpees. We played the Ramones over the van speakers as loud as it would go. We hassled security guards and refused to take cops seriously when they held us up. One night when we were skating in an underground city garage, we found two street cleaners parked. I managed to get both vehicles started. We activated the sweeping brushes and played bumper cars with them until the fuel ran out.

We really didn't miss a single night to be out until the night of Dana's party. The guys made their regular jokes and I pretended to ignore them as usual.

Dana picked me up sometime after nine in her parent's car. I noticed right away that she was wearing lipstick. She caught me looking.

"Like it?"

"I've never seen you wear it before."

"I know, I never do but I thought maybe I would tonight. I can wipe it off."

"No, you don't have to," I looked right at her. "It looks nice."

She smiled. "Thanks."

At the party, Dana stayed with me the whole time and she didn't drink much. It was a similar crowd to the last party I went to with her but this time she just didn't seem that much into it. Her friends tried to convince her to try some mushrooms but she declined and they told her she was lame. She asked if I wanted to leave and I said yes because it sucked worse than last time.

Outside, the temperature was hot and the air humid as we walked along the sidewalk towards the Plymouth. Someone behind us started to make rude comments at Dana. I turned and a guy stepped out of the back lane. He gave me the finger and called Dana a terrible name. He was taller than me and easily weighed seventy pounds more than me in muscle alone. He looked like a football jock.

"Who's your pussy friend?" he asked Dana, still walking towards us.

"None of your business," she replied, trying to act tough, but I could see she was sick with fear.

I whispered to her, asking who this guy was. She took my hand in hers and said nothing. It was then I knew that this was the guy who had raped her.

"You better take off, pussy," he said, glaring at me.

"You touch her and I'll kill you."

He stopped walking towards us. He took out a knife from his jacket pocket.

"Now you can leave superman or I'll give this to ya." He was rolling it around in his hand.

I couldn't make out the guy's face as it was still protected by the shadows of the buildings in the back lane. Suddenly there was a dull thud. The guy fell to his knees and then crashed forward, smacking his face painfully on the concrete. From behind him in the shadows came a short stout figure. It was the Beave. He looked like he was holding an old muffler pipe in his hand. He looked down at his handiwork.

"What a douche!" he said, then looked up at me smiling.

I eventually collected my wits. "What are you doing here?"

"Had some business downtown. You gonna go skate the Edge tomorrow?" He dropped the muffler pipe.

"Yeah," I replied, dumbfounded

"Cool. See you there." He disappeared again down the back lane.

"Who was that?" asked Dana, who was still holding my hand.

"A kid from school. I think."

"Lucky us." She looked at the fallen Goliath on the sidewalk. She walked over to him, fished in his pockets and took his wallet. She opened it and took out sixty dollars, then dropped the wallet between the sewer grates on the street; driver's license, social insurance number, bank card, all of it right down the gutter. You had to hand it to her.

She walked right past me and opened the car door for me.

"Get in."

"Where we going?" I asked

"Just get in."

So I did. She drove off and I watched in the side mirror to see if the guy would get up, but he didn't. He was going to be in rough shape when he finally did come to.

Dana drove us away from downtown and in the direction of Charleswood. We drove beneath the overpass of the perimeter highway and turned into the gravel driveway of an old run down building, parking behind it. In front of us were train tracks with fields of grain fading into the horizon. She got out of the car and told me to do the same. She climbed up on the hood of the car and sat down. I climbed up on the hood beside her.

She took a small mickey from her jacket pocket, unscrewed the top and took a pull. She handed the bottle to me but I waved it off.

"You never drink, huh?" she asked.

"Not really, I can't be drunk and slide hand rails I guess." That was my answer but it never sounded much like the truth, even to me.

"Dana, what are we looking at here?"

"Just be patient," she said, taking another swig and then tucked the bottle back into her pocket.

There was a faint rumble in the distance and then the squealing sound of metal on metal that continued to escalate in volume. I realized Dana had been waiting for a train to come. She reached over and took my hand again as it approached. The noise became much louder and then it was upon us, only mere feet from the front of our car. The sound was deafening. Dana let go of my hand, put her arm around me, leaned in and kissed me. Everything went silent. She moved her hand to the back of my head and I felt her tongue move into my mouth. Then the train was gone and the kiss was over.

"I ruined my lipstick." She was smiling at me, playfully, and then became serious.

"I'm really going to miss you."

"Yeah me too."

She looked like she was going to say something else but didn't. This time I didn't let it pass.

"What?" I asked.

"Nothing." She slid off the hood and I followed her down.

Dana dropped me off at home. We saw each other only once more and only briefly before I left for China. After that I never saw her again.

* * *

I'm forty-one now. I've long since retired from skating after various injuries wouldn't permit me to continue. Sometimes, when a summer day is hot and perfectly peaceful like they can be from time to time, I do look back on that one summer. I think of Terry and building the ramp. I reflect on skating with my brother and the gang. I think of Peter and how the news of his death made me cry one night in China.

I'm married now and have a boy of my own who is about to start high school. He skates and likes to draw like I did, although he's better at the latter than I was and at a much earlier age too. On weekends his friends come over and skate some grind boxes that I built for him in the backyard. Sometimes a girl with dark hair hangs out with them too and I smile when I see him talking to her.

Matthew Cole Joudrey was born on the Isle of Cape Breton. He is a collector of many arcane things and for a time was a professional inline skater. He has lived in almost every Canadian province but due to his affinity for snow and mosquitoes, he moved to Winnipeg where there is an abundance of both. He is married with no cats.

CPSIA information can be obtained at www.ICGtesting.com
235356LV00011B/123/P